THE
STRETFORD
ENDERS

RED FOX Definitions

Also available in **DEFiniTiOnS**

THE STRETFORD ENDERS

TREVOR J. COLGAN

RED FOX DEFinitions

A Red Fox Book

Published by Random House Children's Books
20 Vauxhall Bridge Road, London SW1V 2SA

A division of The Random House Group Ltd
London Melbourne Sydney Auckland
Johannesburg and agencies throughout the world

Text copyright © Trevor J. Colgan 1999

1 3 5 7 9 10 8 6 4 2

First published in Eire
by Praxis Press, 1999

Published in Great Britain
by Red Fox, 2001

MIX
Paper | Supporting
responsible forestry
FSC® C018179

Printed and bound in Great Britain by Clays Ltd, St Ives PLC

THE RANDOM HOUSE GROUP Limited Reg. No. 954009

ISBN 0 09 99409275

contents

For Tony & Bridie Colgan,
James Colgan, Niamh & Jack McMullan.

'Up the Pool.'

i.o.u

Luke Farrell had been robbed by his mother Martina. The decision to move herself and Luke fifteen miles across Dublin, from Rathdale on the northside to Dun Laoghaire on the southside, was down to her promotion at work. Martina had been made junior stock-controller for Boots chemists in Ireland.

Good for Martina. But not for Luke.

Martina would have to train in the main branch of Boots, which was located in Bloomfield shopping centre in Dun Laoghaire. She and Luke would have to move across the Liffey. And that was where the horrors started.

Because it meant Luke would have to leave Rathdale, his home for fourteen years, and start a new life in Dun Laoghaire.

It meant a new school, no friends, a strange place. But most important of all, it meant no league and cup winners' medals.

Because if Luke could just stay in Rathdale for a few more months he was *certain* to win a league and cup double with Rathdale Athletic's under-fourteen football team. He was the only player to play in every game that season. By now the No.7 jersey and the right side of midfield belonged to Luke Farrell.

Martina, of course, knew nothing of this.

Martina didn't know Athletic were eleven points clear at

the top of Dublin Schoolboy Division A. She didn't know they had only six games left to play. She didn't know that they had won their last eight league games on the trot and were unbeaten for four months.

Luke shook his head sadly as he thought of all the other things Martina didn't know about the fortunes of Rathdale Athletic.

She didn't know they had reached the semi-finals of the Coca-Cola All-Ireland Cup without conceding a single goal and that there were still two tough matches to play. And that both these games absolutely required the presence of Luke Farrell if Rathdale Athletic were to get their just reward, the league and cup double.

Well he wouldn't be there now. And Rathdale would go down in ruins without him. All because his mother, Martina, had decided to make something of her life. Fair enough, but she didn't have to go as far as moving to the southside.

Luke stood on the crumbling pavement of Montague Avenue gazing up at Mrs Hendy's house, where Martina had rented the top room overlooking Dublin Bay. Behind him, the blue Ford transit van from Citywide Removals edged away from the kerb and took its place in the heaving tide of traffic slowly moving towards the city centre.

Luke wished he was going north with the van. But the pile of cardboard boxes told him he was stuck on the southside. He put his back to the boxes and gave himself a quick fix by staring out over Dun Laoghaire harbour, across the curved sweep of Dublin Bay to where Howth shimmered in the mist.

Looking left, he squinted hard and could just make out the sandy smudge of Dollymount Strand. Somewhere beyond the strand his heart was buried in a grassy rectangle, flanked by two goalposts and a green container acting as a dressing room. He closed his eyes and imagined Father Collins Park at 11am on a Sunday morning.

He could see Mr O Driscoll, Athletic's manager, decked out in his lucky green wellies, cheering on the lads from the touchline. He could see Anto Morris, Athletic's inspirational captain, clapping his hands together and shouting 'C'mon lads,' to encourage his team-mates. He could see himself, racing down the right wing with the ball at his feet, skipping round the desperate tackle of the left-full before swinging across a perfect centre for Alan Kidd to head home. 1–0 to Rathdale Athletic.

Luke opened his eyes. He didn't want to think about Rathdale Athletic any more. It only made things worse. He crouched down, lifted up the final cardboard box from the pavement, pushed in the wrought-iron gate, and made his way through the front garden and up the granite steps.

Even in his gloom, Luke knew that Mrs Hendy's three storey house at 8 Montague Avenue had once been a fine building. Martina was mad about it, said it was a Regency house, whatever that was, and that it had great character. And, although it looked slightly shabby, he was glad it wasn't painted horrible purple, brown, or custard yellow like the other six houses in the short terrace. Mrs Hendy's house was a faded salmon pink. Like an Everton away jersey from 1992 that was still being worn well past its sell-by date.

At the top of the five granite steps was a big dark-green door with a cast-iron gargoyle doorknob and a fanlight above. Luke had left it open and now he nudged it shut softly behind him with his shoulder blade as he stepped in. He had a feeling that in Mrs Hendy's house the sound of slamming doors was seldom heard.

As the door closed behind him with a solid clunk, the light failed to pass through the dusty fanlight and the hallway was shrouded in gloom. There was a strong smell of polish and old wood.

Luke manoeuvred his box past the huge hallstand with some difficulty. The ghostly fronds of a gloomy plant in a brass pot brushed his face as he passed.

At the far end of the hall was a closed door. Luke knew Mrs Hendy lived behind it so he tried to step softly as he made his way to the staircase. Mrs Hendy had made it clear, when she'd laid down the house rules to Martina, that she didn't like a lot of noise.

Luke didn't like the little he had seen of Mrs Hendy. She seemed stiff and severe. But Martina didn't seem to mind her. She said that Mrs Hendy was not your normal landlady, just someone who had seen better times and could just about bear to take in two tenants.

Luke reached the top of the first staircase and rested the box on the seat of a tall window. He stared down at the back garden. It was a walled garden, long and narrow. A path of flat stepping stones wound from the crumbling conservatory, at the back of the house, across a small lawn, among herbaceous borders and disappeared out of sight beneath a willow overhanging a garden pond. Beyond the willow he thought he saw what might have been a green painted wooden shed, but he couldn't be sure.

Luke mentally measured the lawn and felt the foundation of a smile appear on his face. 'Perfect for footie,' he thought to himself. The only problem being, he had no one to play with.

Luke turned away from the window. He climbed the second staircase leaning onto the second landing where their rooms were. Leaning the cardboard box against the wall with one hand, he turned the heavy old key in the door and pushed it wide open.

Light blazed towards Luke from the two tall windows

overlooking Dublin Bay. Even in his depression, the sight gave Luke a lift. He set the box in the centre of the spacious room and looked around. Through a door he could see a small compact kitchen. The bathroom was on the landing outside – the only drawback that Martina had mentioned. But he had his own small bedroom off the kitchen. And of course, the magnificent main living room from which he could always see his beloved northside.

Luke looked at the cardboard pyramid waiting to be unpacked. And felt his heart sink again. There were fifteen separate cardboard boxes, packed with their possessions, lying on the faded rose carpet. Everything he and Martina had in the whole world.

He opened the first box and took out his football boots.

'Ma,' Luke said.

He made his way down the staircase slowly. As he moved closer to the ground floor, the hallway started to sink into darkness. It reflected Luke's mood perfectly.

'Ma,' he said, calling louder this time.

The ground floor was still and silent. The only noise Luke could hear was the muffled but rhythmic rumble of a Dart moving in or out of Dun Laoghaire train station. He moved to Mrs Hendy's door and turned the knob without thinking. He stared into the parlour. Martina and Mrs Hendy looked at him over two teacups.

'Luke,' Martina said in disgust. 'What did I say about knocking on doors and waiting for an answer?'

Luke stood inside the doorway feeling foolish. He knew he had broken one of the ground rules. But he still felt Martina was treating him unfairly. She could have brought it up when they were on their own. He felt she was making a public point to impress Mrs Hendy.

'Sorry,' he said sulkily.

Mrs Hendy looked at Luke for a long time. He waited for her to make a meal out of his mother's remark but she just put down her teacup quietly. She stared out at the garden, giving Luke his first good look at her.

She sat as erect as a soldier. Her silvery white hair was cut short. She wore an old tailored jacket with a plain white blouse, sensible black shoes and steel spectacles with black cords dangling below each lens. There was something sad in those sharp blue eyes behind the spectacles.

Martina gave a gentle cough. 'Can we talk about the rent, Mrs Hendy?' she said. Mrs Hendy flushed slightly. 'Yes, I suppose we must.'

She got up and walked across to the fireplace, picked up a soot-covered poker and prodded the dying embers of the fire.

'Will you need a deposit?' Martina asked carefully.

'No, no need for that,' Mrs Hendy said.

Luke lost interest in the rent discussion. He was busy looking around the room. For such a big room there wasn't much furniture. A sprawling old sofa and two leather armchairs – now occupied by Mrs Hendy and Martina – faced the marble fireplace. A writing desk stood in an alcove near the fire. A big bookcase filled the back wall facing the French windows that led to the garden. And in front of the window stood an old piano.

Luke moved to the piano. A faded photograph in a silver frame stood alone on the top. Smiling out at him were two young men and two young women. The men wore pilots' caps with flaps, flying goggles pushed high, and white scarves round their necks.

Even in a black and white photograph the girls looked sunny in summer dresses. Behind them he could see part of the fuselage cockpit of a small fighter with what looked like a painted bullseye.

Luke knew he was looking at a Second World War Spitfire. He had seen them often enough in old comics and once in a black and white newsreel about the Battle of Britain. He wondered who the people in the picture were.

Beside the photograph stood a small wooden box. Luke glanced at his mother and Mrs Hendy, still droning on, and lifted the lid with one finger. Inside was a medal in the form of a cross, and beside it some faded red flowers.

'Leave those things alone Luke!' said his mother sharply.

Luke turned. Martina gave him a look. But Mrs Hendy didn't seem to mind. She glanced from him to the photograph and stared out the window. Martina watched her for a moment and spoke gently as if not wishing to break into a memory.

'So the last day of the month, Mrs Hendy,' Martina said, getting to her feet.

'Yes, yes,' Mrs Hendy said quickly. She got to her feet too and showed them to the door. Just before she closed it she spoke quickly. 'And of course the boy can play in the garden whenever he wishes.'

Martina looked at Luke with a smile.

'Thank you, Mrs Hendy,' she said. But the door was already closed.

Martina remained silent all the way up to the second landing. Luke was worried that she was employing a 'Wait till I get you home' routine. But when she had unlocked the front door, she turned towards Luke and surprised him.

'How about McDonalds for dinner?'

Luke looked at her suspiciously and nodded his head in agreement.

Martina advanced on him, wrapping her arms round his shoulders.

'Ma,' he said, struggling in protest. As a teenage boy, Luke considered it his job, nay his duty, to moan in embarrassment whenever his mother showed such signs of affection.

In the mock struggle something fell from his hand to the floor. Martina picked it up. The red paper flower.

'Where did you get the poppy?' she said.

'From Mrs Hendy's box,' said Luke. 'I forgot I was still holding it.'

Martina studied the paper flower for a moment.

'My grandfather used to wear one of these every November,' she said flatly. 'No matter what people said.'

Luke looked curiously at her set face.

'Why would they say anything?'

Martina got her coat, still with that closed expression.

'Ireland was neutral in the War. People who wore poppies were called West Brits.'

'What's a West Brit?' said Luke.

Martina sighed. 'Why don't you ask me easy stuff like where do babies come from?' she said.

Luke would have liked a chat about that too. But not with his mother. And certainly not while he was eating a Big Mac.

WE LIVE IN DUN LAOGHAIRE

Luke stood on the pedestrian walkway between O'Reilly's pub and Bloomfield shopping centre. It was half eight in the evening and night had fallen. A freezing February breeze, straight from the North sea, whipped over Dun Laoghaire harbour and cut across his face, forcing him to turn slightly to the left.

Luke sucked hard to extract the last droplets of his chocolate milkshake. Martina caught up beside him and they both glanced in at the illuminated shop window of the Bloomfield Centre.

'Well, now we know where everything is,' Martina said brightly.

Luke allowed a few seconds to pass before asking sarcastically, 'We don't know where "Woodlawn" Comprehensive is.'

Martina stared at him. He had made a point of pronouncing the word Woodlawn in a snobby southside accent. Martina held on to her tiny grin, desperate not to encourage his dislike of Dun Laoghaire.

'It's only five minutes from here,' she said brightly.

The shop to the right of Boots Chemists caught Luke's attention. Barnes' Sports Store. He walked across to the shop window and glanced in at the football jerseys.

Manchester United's new away kit took pride of place, along with United scarves, T-shirts, coffee mugs, key-rings and souvenir clocks. But there was no sign of Celtic jerseys, or Liverpool, or Arsenal, or Villa, or Spurs, but worst of all, no Everton . . .

'Do Everton have a new jersey out?' Martina asked.

Luke felt she was making conversation to kill time.

'No.'

'Let's go, Luke,' Martina said softly. 'The school's only five minutes from here.'

Luke took a last look at the biased display in Barnes' window. To the far left of the Man Utd shrine was a black and white framed photograph hanging on the wall behind the shop counter. It was a junior football team lined up in two rows, one standing, one kneeling. Their manager or coach stood beside them proudly, a massive figure in a black tracksuit.

Luke squinted hard to read the inscription below the photo. The something Enders, season 1998/99.

'Luke,' Martina called loudly.

She had broken his concentration.

'I'm coming.' He replied impatiently.

When Luke turned back to the shop window he almost jumped in terror. A face stared back at him from the darkened shop floor. A tall black man eyed him suspiciously.

Luke back-pedalled nervously. He turned away to follow his mother. The wind whistled. He felt that if it was longer than five minutes he would get frostbite.

The walk from the shopping centre to Woodlawn Comprehensive school took a full twenty minutes. Luke didn't look at his mother for the last fifteen. And Martina saved her breath for the uphill slog.

Finally they were there. Locked out. Luke stood beneath the orange glare of a street-lamp, staring at the locked school gates in disgust. Martina shrugged her shoulders.

'I thought it was a five-minute walk, tops,' she said innocently.

Luke could have made a thousand smart-arse comments about the difference in time between his and his mother's journeys to work and school. But he had no heart for it. Not with Woodlawn Comprehensive waiting for him in the darkness.

He walked up to the black iron gates. He placed his hands on the bars as if he were inside a prison cell. He peered along the winding driveway which led to the main school building a hundred yards away.

It was the usual boring modern building. The walls were a chalky white colour, blotted with big brutal windows, as if the place doubled as a pillbox in a war film. In front of the building three tarmac basketball courts lay side by side. A few oak trees threw sinister shadows. Not a pretty sight. But wait . . .

Luke leaned his head hard against the bars and squinted to make sure. Yes. Behind all the basketball rubbish a full length football pitch stretched itself in the shadow of the main building.

Luke let out a little sigh of relief.

'Everything OK?' Martina said.

Luke dug his hands deep into his jacket pockets.

'I suppose so,' he said neutrally. Like Ireland in the War.

Luke clamped the metal zipper on his jacket between his teeth. He turned away from the gates and headed back down Woodlawn Drive.

Martina smiled to herself as she watched him go. The first thing she had noticed on her way in to see Mr O'Shea the principal was the football pitch, and she knew all along that it would be the first thing Luke would spot.

Martina caught up with Luke at the bottom of Patrick

Street. She jabbed the button at the pedestrian crossing. They waited for the little green man to appear as a convoy of Landrovers and BMWs headed for Dalkey.

The task of settling into life in Dun Laoghaire had always seemed pretty straightforward to Martina. Learning to cope with her new job and college would more than fill the void for her. Now she felt confident that Woodlawn Comprehensive school would help fill the void for Luke.

She glanced sideways at Luke. He was hunched deep in his tracksuit top. He looked totally miserable. And she knew inside that the only way to fill the void in Luke was to take a Dart back to the northside.

She sighed silently. For a moment she almost weakened and wondered if she should call Jay. A boy needed his father. She watched the lights change. And suddenly smiled.

Nobody needed a little green man like Jay.

Then she squared her shoulders, put her hand on Luke's shoulders, whether he liked it or not, and marched straight into the north-easterly blowing across the bay.

THE FIRST FEW DAYS

It was the last thing Luke, or any other kid in the whole wide world, wanted on his or her first day in a new school. But Martina had insisted on walking to the school gates with him. All along Woodlawn Drive, Luke ran the gauntlet of giggles and smirks.

He had only been in Woodlawn Comprehensive a minute and already complete strangers, people he had never met before in his life, were laughing at him. Could things get any worse?

Stupid question. At the school gates Martina planted a kiss on Luke's forehead. He struggled to free himself from her loving embrace and finally succeeded, fleeing to the safety of the school grounds.

Martina continued to wave proudly as Luke sank his head towards his Nike Air runners and ran along like a rat.

'Bye, darling,' she said loudly.

Luke didn't reply with a single word, gesture or movement. He kept his head down in a low bow and walked quickly along the tarmac driveway towards the main building.

'Bye, darling,' a boy's voice said intimately.

Luke gave a fast furtive look. He was surrounded by blank faces. Everyone within fifty feet of him on the driveway had heard Martina's call of goodbye, but no one had the guts to slag him to his face. Yet. They waited for Luke's head to bow towards the ground.

As soon as it did the endearments started again. A gushy voice playing Martina. 'Bye Bye, darling.' And the oily voice playing him. 'Bye, Mummy.' And everybody improvising around them and making disgusting wet kissing sounds. 'I luv youuuuu.'

Luke let out a quiet groan of despair. He kept his eyes locked on the laces of his trainers. After such a disastrous start to life in Woodlawn Comprehensive, the most important thing to do now was to slink into the background and become totally invisible and inconspicuous.

'Let's hear it for Luke Farrell!!!'

Silence. Luke hung his head between Mr O'Shea, the principal, and Mr Duffy, the class tutor. He hoped death would come soon.

2C knew that they would have to make an effort soon. But not just yet. Let the northside git sweat on the cross first.

Mr O'Shea frowned. 'Now fair's fair. Luke's mother has moved herself and Luke all the way to Dun Laoghaire to take up a new job.'

Several of the class sniggered. But Mr Duffy who was built like an Army Ranger, sucked his teeth and stared at the ring-leader.

'Shut up, Swayne,' he said softly.

Swayne, a thickset boy, shut up. Mr O'Shea gave Mr Duffy a grateful glance.

'Now 2C, let's have a warm round of applause for your new friend Luke Farrell.'

Luke tried hard not to cringe as his new classmates gave him a sterile round of applause. Every student in 2C stared up at him with obvious contempt. A bug-eyed alien, Gary Barlow, Darth Vader, even a man-eating grizzly bear would have received a warmer reception.

The only friendly face belonged to a cute girl with long curly blonde hair sitting at the top of the class. Luke smiled back.

'Take a seat, Luke,' Mr Duffy said.

Luke picked his royal blue Umbro schoolbag off the floor. He moved down the room, carefully stepping over the feet stretched in his path, bumping into only one desk on the way. So far so good.

The blonde girl smiled his way. The boy Mr Duffy called Swayne was sitting beside her, a handsome muscle-bound thug with jet-black hair. He wore a stern expression. He stared straight into Luke's eyes and spoke through his teeth like a ventriloquist.

'Honchee.'

Luke decided to stand his ground.

'Piss off,' he replied as he walked past the table.

Swayne threw out his left leg in an attempt to send Luke crashing to the floor. But Luke had had lots of experience evading the desperate tackles of full-backs. He swayed sideways and Swayne was left sliding down on his seat, dangerously over-extended.

'Don't get smart, Honchee,' Swayne puffed as he sat up.

Luke glanced at the blonde girl. Somehow he expected her to come to his defence. She didn't. She helped Swayne to sit up.

Mr Duffy tapped the desk as Mr O'Shea rolled from the room.

'Chop-chop, Luke,' he said.

Luke was running out of space. There was only one place left to sit. At the back of the room, at a desk on her own, sat a black girl with long braided hair wearing chunky glasses, bleached blue denim dungarees, wine Doc Martins and a navy duffel jacket.

'There's a free seat beside Ella,' Mr Duffy said.

Ella moved a millimetre to her left. Luke had little option. He slung his bag beneath the table and sat down beside her. Ella moved another millimetre away. No go there either.

Luke took out his Everton FC pencil-case. Mr Duffy was writing on the blackboard, back to the class. Swayne turned and hissed savagely down the room.

'Honchee.'

Luke felt the black girl give him a glance. Was she waiting for him to stand up to Swayne? No way. Not until he had sussed out the level of Swayne's support. He bent over his book.

But his brain was boiling. Two days in Dun Laoghaire and already enemies were mounting. He would have to lie low and bury himself in schoolwork. What other way to escape the nightmare of Woodlawn Comprehensive School?

This didn't prove a problem in Mr Duffy's history class. He was an excellent teacher. His first lesson was about World War Two. He explained how Hitler had killed six million Jews. And how Ireland and Sweden remained neutral throughout the war.

Luke didn't understand how anyone could stay neutral. If he had been alive in 1940 he would have wanted to fight against the Nazis. Maybe this was what the West Brits did, the people who wore the red paper flowers.

Martina said West Brits were Irish people who went off to join the British army to fight against Germany.

'What was wrong with fighting Hitler?' Luke thought to himself.

For the next two days Luke stuck to his plan. Don't stand out. In every class he ended up sitting beside Ella. She never spoke to him. In fact she never spoke to anybody. So you could say he was on an equal footing where Ella was concerned. At the bottom with everybody else.

By Wednesday morning Luke was becoming accustomed to the various names and faces in 2C. He soon found out that the blonde girl with the friendly smile was Cecilia Giles.

Cecilia was the main attraction. She was constantly swarmed by a gang of girls who seemed to hang on her every word. Pretending to be preoccupied with a Concern poster asking for volunteers in Somalia – which he felt would be only marginally more miserable than Dun Laoghaire – Luke listened in to their conversation outside French class.

From the snippets he picked up, it seemed that Cecilia would soon be performing on the TV talent show, *Star Search 2000*. It appeared to be only the first step in what her friends agreed would be a stunningly successful career.

Starting with *Star Search*, Cecilia would act, sing and dance her way throughout the world, making the sun shine on TV3, re-working Riverdance, presenting the MTV Music Awards. Cecilia had big ambitions. And Swayne would always be in the audience.

Before each class, 2C would surround Cecilia or Swayne, who would then conduct the conversation. There was a definite order of importance, and everyone seemed to know their place. When to talk, and when to listen.

For the boys, the time to talk was when Swayne stopped talking, and the only thing they needed to do was laugh or agree with whatever he had just said. For the girls, the required response to a story from Cecilia was to act as if it were the most amazing thing they had ever heard.

Luke noticed that Ella was the only girl who refused to take part in the daily grooming of Cecilia and Swayne. Ella walked from class to class alone, either listening to her Walkman or reading from her Manchester City magazine.

Luke also wanted to know more about Tonka Matthews, a blocky boy who stayed away from the pack who sucked up to Swayne. Tonka was built like a truck. And even Swayne and his cronies stood aside when Tonka Matthews had the hammer down.

Although they had never spoken, Luke somehow felt safer when Tonka was around. He looked across the corridor now to where Tonka was leaning against the wall listening to his Walkman.

Tonka was wearing a full-length green army jacket, dark brown hair down to the small of his back, headphones audibly crackling with ear-piercing heavy metal. The small yellow schoolbag slung from his shoulder was scribbled with black biro signs that he was not to be messed with: Motorhead, Slayer, Iron Maiden and Soundgarden.

'Hey, Honchee, where did you rob those runners?' Swayne said suddenly and loudly into Luke's left ear.

Swayne and his cronies laughed. 2C watched and waited, standing well back from Luke with the mob's instinct for the wounded animal. Luke looked round for any allies.

Ella leaned against the wall, only ten feet away from her classmates. Like Tonka, she too was tuned into her Walkman and tuned out of Luke's life. No help there.

Cecilia and the girls looked at Luke like cats. They smelled blood. Luke hoped it wouldn't be his. But he knew nobody else was betting that way. Sooner or later Swayne would force a confrontation. He was a bully, and he would never show Luke mercy as long as he had an advantage.

'Hey, Honchee.' Swayne almost sang the words.

2C laughed like a studio audience. Ella went on reading her magazine. Tonka turned up the volume on his Walkman. Metallic sounds filled the space. Swayne smiled like a shark. He knew he had the entire class on his side. The attack would continue to gain momentum unless the teacher showed up soon.

Luke scanned his classmates' faces for one friendly glance. Nothing. Cecilia stared straight into his eyes, smiling at him, not with him, waiting to see how it would work out.

Just as well she stayed on the sideline. If Swayne noticed Cecilia giving Luke a supportive look it could cause him to erupt with jealousy. Luke knew this, Swayne knew this, but no one knew this better than Cecilia.

So now it was clear. She and Swayne were an item. But if Luke could survive, *he* and she might become an item. Mad dream.

'Don't worry, Honchee, I can speak fluent northside,' Swayne said.

2C laughed again. But Luke noticed that Cecilia remained silent. She was having an each way bet. Another blonde neutral country. She could have played Sweden in the War, Luke thought sarcastically.

But there was no neutrality where he was. Swayne was pacing about his classmates like the picture of Hitler walking amongst the Wehrmacht in the history book. It was only a matter of time before he saw that Cecilia was not totally committed to the Swayne side. When he did, he would blame Luke and that would make matters a lot worse. So Luke tried not to look at Cecilia. Unfortunately he found himself looking at Swayne.

Swayne snarled and stood toe to toe, looking into Luke's eyes. He was at least six inches taller.

'Looking at something, Honchee?' he said quietly.

Luke stared back at Swayne. He was seconds away from a nasty punch-up. Whatever he said now would earn him a blow. For a shameful moment he felt like crying. And then he stiffened his back and prepared to go down without a sound.

'Leave him alone, penis-breath.'

Luke stared in shock. Swayne swung round in a rage.

Ella was still leaning against the wall, flicking through her magazine. But from the way the class watched her in horror it was clear that it was she who had spoken.

Swayne took a step towards her.

'Did you say something, spade?' he hissed.

2C watched Ella with bated breath.

'Yes. I said leave him alone, penis-breath,' Ella said without looking up.

Luke stared at her in awe. A silence. Then suddenly 2C started to laugh. At Swayne. Luke looked around, amazed. Swayne's cronies, carried away, were laughing too. And it was contagious. In a second the whole corridor was rocking. Tonka took off his headphones so he could join in.

Luke had just got in his own first laugh when Miss Court arrived to spoil what was shaping up as his first good day in Dun Laoghaire.

'Chop-chop, 2C,' she said.

Miss Court strode inside. Luke stood by the door as if on guard. Nobody moved. Everybody looked at Ella. Swayne sensed the strange mood of the class and stayed silent. Cecilia stared at the scene, confused.

Ella took her time. She tucked her headphones into her bag and walked to where Luke was waiting.

'Thanks,' he said softly.

Ella gave him an enigmatic glance and walked past him to take her seat. Only then did the rest of 2C make a move. Swayne slung his black Puma King schoolbag over his shoulder and strode inside the classroom, scowling at Ella before subsiding into his seat.

Ten minutes into the class, as 2C jotted down notes from

the blackboard about conjugating the French verb 'to go', Luke whispered to Ella.

'Thanks again.'

Ella looked across at Luke briefly. 'I heard you the first time.'

They stared at one another for half a second.

Then Ella went back to her note-taking. The remaining half hour of the French class passed off in complete silence. Ella hardly looked his way. But Swayne made sure to stare across at her every five minutes. It was an obvious scare tactic, aimed at unnerving Ella. It didn't work. She paid no attention to Swayne. Luke, however, was becoming concerned. As the bell rang out for lunch-time, Luke darted his eyes between Ella, Swayne and his cronies carefully.

Ella had packed her bag and was heading up the aisle. Swayne readied himself to stick out a foot. But Luke timed his interception perfectly. He cut in front of Ella. Swayne couldn't resist trying for a trip. And this time Luke let himself go down. But he was careful to sprawl all over Swayne as he did so.

'Gerroff, Honchee!'

Ella stepped round the mess. She looked down at Luke.

'Thanks,' she said.

Swayne clawed Luke away. Contenting himself with a casual dig he made his way out of the room with Niall Casey. Luke took his time, slowly packing his books and pencil-case in case they were waiting outside. As soon as Miss Court made a move he tried to use her as cover. But Casey buttonholed him outside the door as if he had something important to ask him about the French homework. As soon as Miss Court was gone, Swayne kicked Luke's left ankle and issued a little warning.

'Don't push your luck, Honchee.'

Swayne, Casey and his five cronies marched off. Luke crouched down to zip up his scattered schoolbag.

'You forgot this,' a sweet voice said.

Luke looked up at Cecilia. She held out an orange pencil.

'Nice one,' Luke said. And saw straightaway that his northside slang caused her eyes to cloud over.

Their fingers grazed. He fought hard not to gulp with excitement. Cecilia smiled at him, revealing her perfectly maintained pearly white teeth.

'See you later,' she said effortlessly.

'Bye,' Luke replied.

He watched Cecilia walk, well, almost skip down the corridor. Her curly blonde hair jiggled up and down playfully on her shoulders. She took advantage of Woodlawn's lax approach to school uniform, wearing a soft pink sweater with cream pedal-pushers. 'It's the middle of winter,' Luke thought to himself. 'She must be freezing.' His mind went blank. A new thought breezed in. 'Who cares?'

Luke got to his feet, picked up his schoolbag and headed towards the exit. He walked on air. Cecilia and Luke.

So why was he thinking of Ella?

Martina insisted Luke spend his first lunch hour with her. Of course in mother language this translated into spend 'their' first lunch hour 'together'. However, it was Luke who had to walk for twenty minutes to meet Martina outside McDonalds in Dun Laoghaire town centre. And of course their 'first lunch-hour together' had soon stretched into 'every lunch-hour together'.

Luke hadn't minded the long lunches much on Monday and Tuesday. But today was Wonderful Wednesday. He listened to Martina babbling about her day with ill-concealed impatience.

Wonderingly, he found himself wishing he was back at school, not eating a Big Mac. Woodlawn was where the action was. Swayne was still a serious threat but somehow Cecilia and Ella balanced that. Amazingly he found he wanted to get back to the battlefield.

He worked his way swiftly through the entire meal of Big Mac, large fries and strawberry milkshake while Martina gave him another instalment of her working life. Luke had been getting this in episodes, like a soap. In three days they had covered such topics as her new office, how nice the staff were, and the foibles of Mr Foley, the senior stock-controller.

Amanda was the star of today's story. An old friend from Boots in Coolock Shopping Centre, it seemed that Amanda had also been working in the Bloomfield branch until last month when she had left to become manager of Dixons Electrical Store. As he listened to Martina babbling away about all this, Luke wondered if his mother had lost her mind.

'Luke, you're not listening,' she said sadly.

When Luke reached the gates of Woodlawn Comprehensive on Thursday afternoon, the school grounds were full with students basking in the unseasonably warm weather. Scorching sunshine was a rare enough sight in the height of an Irish summer. Its presence in the middle of February seemed like a case for Mulder and Scully.

Small groups of students sat around in circles on the grass. Luke noticed Cecilia holding court with her friends behind the football pitch. She smiled across at Luke, who waved his hand in a nervous reply. Cecilia laughed, one of her friends whispered in her ear, the other girls looked across at Luke, they were laughing too. Luke was too far away to hear what was so funny.

He glanced about the school yard. Three separate basket-ball games were in progress. Some other students were eating sweets, chatting, locking their bikes up, listening to their Walkmans.

Beneath the shade of a large oak tree, far off in the left corner of the school grounds, Ella sat alone, reading. Luke stared across at her for a while, there wasn't another student within fifty feet of her. From a distance it was a gloomy pic-ture. But there was something about Ella. She didn't seem the sort of person who needed people. She was a loner, happy with her thoughts. At least it seemed that way to Luke.

'Honchee,' a voice called.

A leather football swooped past Luke's left ear. He turned round. Casey was standing on the goal-line of the football pitch. He wanted the ball back. Luke jogged forward, per-formed a Cruyff flick to get the ball in front of him, then smacked it back to Casey. No sign of a thank you. Casey took a goal kick. Luke sat down in the grass and started to watch the match.

Swayne, Casey, five of his cronies, or Co as Luke liked to call them, and some other boys from 2C formed the blue team. The reds were made up of other second years and some smaller first year boys. Luke concentrated on Swayne's per-formance. He played as a centre-half. He wasn't very skilful, but he managed to use physical strength to muscle opponents off the ball.

The overall level of play was pretty awful. No one looked to pass the ball along the ground. They seemed content to whack it into the air, Wimbledon style. Luke watched the game for fifteen minutes, in which time, both teams man-aged a pathetic two shots on target. Full-time was called by Mr O'Shea and the ding-ding of his trusty brass school-bell.

As Luke walked towards the main building he noticed Ella

was already at the door. Cecilia and her gang made a four-course meal of getting to their feet, while the footballers gathered their schoolbags from behind the goal and discussed the highlights of the game.

Luke almost smiled. But at the same time, he wanted to cry. It occurred to him his life was divided between Woodlawn Comprehensive, Montague Avenue and Bloomfield Shopping Centre. He had only been away a week but already Rathdale was becoming a memory.

He found himself looking forward to his second week in Woodlawn.

ADAPTING

Luke's first week in Woodlawn Comprehensive had been eventful. The next five were incredibly dull. It seemed the adventure of 'a new school' lasted as long as the taste in a stick of chewing gum. School had settled back to being school. A place Luke never wanted to be, but somewhere he had to go.

'Bye, Luke,' Cecilia said.

Luke sat at his table in room eleven, packing away his History book, refill pad and pencil case. 2C had just finished classes for Friday afternoon. Cecilia drifted past Luke's table, flanked by her gang of followers.

'Bye,' he replied.

Luke turned around to check on Swayne. He was at the bottom of the class with Co. More importantly, he was unaware of Luke's verbal exchange with Cecilia. Luke blew out a quiet sigh of relief. Yet another close shave. Ella slung her schoolbag over her shoulder and got to her feet, giving Luke a second-long glance.

'You're just a pawn in her game,' Ella said.

Luke watched Ella walk out of room eleven and down the corridor. He was in two minds whether to follow her. He decided against it.

It was a cold and rainy afternoon outside, more becoming of a typical day in February. Luke kept a close eye on the students in front of him on the driveway. He wanted to avoid a chance encounter with Cecilia and her gang. Her amorous smiles and waves had continued all through the weeks. It was only a matter of time before Swayne blew a fuse. Then it was a fight, a fight Luke had no chance to win.

'Don't rob any cars on the way home, Honchee,' Swayne said, shouting.

Luke glanced behind him. Swayne and Co stood beneath the corrugated iron roof of the bike shed laughing. It was easy to be funny with a gang of lick-arses around you. Luke smiled back at Swayne, then held his thumb aloft.

'Dick,' Luke said quietly as he walked towards the school gates.

Dealing with verbal abuse was one thing, physical violence was quite another. It wasn't that Luke was scared of fighting Swayne. The problem lay in the odds he would face. Co would hardly stand by and let Luke get the better of Swayne, if he happened to get the better of him.

Luke pulled the hood of his rainjacket over his head as the rain began to pelt down heavily on Woodlawn Drive. He cut across the road and headed through Woodlawn Park, turning left past the burnt out Nissan Micra into Woodlawn housing estate.

Over the course of his first full week in school Luke had done a bit of exploring. Thanks to a couple of creative short-cuts he had shaved ten minutes off his walk home. It would have been good news, if there was anything worth going home for.

Luke opened the front door. He slung his schoolbag on the floor and walked straight across to the fridge. Martina had left a note on the freezer door.

Stock-take tonight.
Pizza inside.

I'll be home at 11pm,
Love, Mum.

Luke sighed. He opened the freezer door and pulled out the Goodfellas deep-pan pepperoni pizza. So far, Martina had been home for tea once. Her degree in Information Technology meant she had classes four nights a week, Monday to Thursday. Friday was stock-take night in Boots and Saturday was late opening till 9pm.

Luke turned on the oven and walked across to the kitchen table. Boots had allowed Martina to borrow an old Packard Bell PC from the office to help her with her degree in Information Technology. Luke clicked the ON switch on the hard drive. As Windows 95 loaded, he walked into his bedroom.

Rain drizzled against the window pane. A puffy screen of condensation blocked his view of dreary Montague Avenue. It was a cold, horrible day, but even if the sun were scorching through the glass, Luke would be wary about going outside. The only time he'd ventured outside Mrs Hendy's boarding house, apart from trips to and from school, was that first night in McDonalds.

Instead, Luke always came home from school, cooked his frozen pizza or microwaved his frozen lasagne. Then settled down in front of the Packard Bell PC and played *Championship Manager 2* all night.

Luke had two separate games running on the computer. In one he was managing Everton. The year was 1998, Luke's first season in charge. They were currently fifth in the Premiership and faced a home tie with Tottenham Hotspur in the quarter-finals of the FA Cup.

The other game was with the Republic of Ireland, where Luke had brought the boys in green to the brink of qualification for World Cup 2002 in Japan. All they required to be sure of a place in the finals was a point in the last game at home to Belgium.

Luke got into his Adidas tracksuit bottoms and his Everton jersey. He wandered back into the living room, wiped the condensation from the window and glanced out at drizzly south Dublin.

The street lights on Montague Avenue were burning a bright, vibrant yellow. Beyond these lights, the pitch black pool of Dublin Bay was illuminated by a loose line of flickering orange lights that circled the coastline in the shape of a horseshoe.

Luke had lost all track of time. Ireland had gained the single point they needed thanks to a last minute Ian Harte penalty in a dramatic 2–2 draw with Belgium. It meant a trip to the World Cup Finals.

Ireland were drawn in Group C with Germany, Bolivia and The Ivory Coast. After a season of friendly games to prepare, Luke began the World Cup without his main strike partnership of Robbie Keane and Keith O'Neill, who were both suspended. The first group match against Germany finished in a disappointing 4–1 defeat.

The result left Ireland needing at least a point against Bolivia to have any chance of qualifying for the second round. Boosted by the return of Keane and O'Neill, Ireland turned on the style and thrashed Bolivia 3–0.

It meant the last game against The Ivory Coast was all or nothing. Despite a horrific first half, going 2–0 behind and having Richard Dunne sent off for a professional foul, Ireland retrieved the match with an astonishing second-half hat-trick from Robbie Keane.

In the second round Ireland were drawn to face Portugal,

who had won Group D from Argentina with ease. Luke had a crucial decision to make: changing to a 4–5–1 defensive formation to try and stifle the talented Portuguese forwards, or keeping faith with Keane and O'Neill up front with an attacking 4–4–2.

Luke chewed his bottom lip as he stared at the screen, mulling over the decision. His concentration was broken by the sound of muffled laughter and approaching footsteps in the hallway. Martina was outside the door.

'Luke,' Martina said as she opened the door.

'What?' he replied moodily, without looking her way.

Martina walked in, unruffled by his sulky reply. A tall blonde woman followed after her. They each carried a bottle of wine wrapped in a brown paper bag.

'Amanda, you remember my charming son, Luke,' Martina said.

Amanda stared at Luke for a moment, a saucy grin of shock and surprise on her face. Luke began to feel rather self-conscious. His cheeks reddened and he looked away in embarrassment. Amanda strode forward and brushed her fingers through Luke's chestnut brown hair.

'Oh my god, you've grown so big,' she said, smiling.

Martina opened the cupboard above the fridge. She took two wine glasses out and placed them on the counter.

'The only thing that's grown is his mouth,' Martina said sarcastically.

Amanda ignored this comment, she examined Luke with a mix of pride and surprise. She took hold of his right cheek between her thumb and forefinger.

'Don't mind her,' Amanda said.

She pulled Luke's head close to her large breasts and kissed him on his crown. Martina opened a bottle of wine and poured two glasses.

Spurred on by a reckless abandon and optimism inspired by the presence of Amanda O'Reilly, Luke decided to stick with his attacking 4–4–2 formation and play Keane and O'Neill up front. It was an inspired gamble. Portugal hit the woodwork four times, Figo missed a penalty but Ireland still ran out 2–1 winners. It meant a quarter-final showdown with Italy.

While Luke pondered who should replace the injured Stephan Carr at right-back for the game against the Italians, Martina and Amanda drank wine and caught up on old times. Luke earwigged, naturally, but soon enough wished he hadn't.

Amanda had no shortage of men lining up to date her. Within two hours and a bottle and a half of white wine, Amanda had told Martina (and Luke) about fourteen men she had dated since moving to Dun Laoghaire in 1997. Her busy social life was based around The Wicked Wolf pub in Blackrock and the Inferno nightclub on the Morehampton Road.

Amanda had worked her way through a string of bankers, architects, doctors, and self-made businessmen. The affluent pubs and nightclubs of southside Dublin were the perfect ponds to fish in for a husband with the wealth to make your life a luxurious stroll. Amanda seemed prepared to throw back the smaller fish and hold out for a bite from the great white shark.

'I don't know how you do it,' Martina said sadly.

Luke stuck his head out from behind the PC monitor for a brief second. Amanda and Martina, shoes off, were snuggled up on the couch, sipping wine. Luke took another look at his mother. She ran her baby finger round the rim of the wine glass. There was no disguising the unhappiness in her large green eyes.

'What are you talking about?' Amanda said. 'You could have anyone you want.'

Martina laughed sadly. 'Yeah, I can see them queuing up from here to Rathdale.'

This was a shock to the system for Luke. It was the first time he had considered the possibility of his mother feeling lonely. She had been on her own since Jay left them. That was seven years ago, a long time for anyone.

Luke looked at Martina again. This time he tried to look at her as an ordinary woman, not his mother. Even from his own biased point of view, Martina was beautiful. Thirty-one years of age. Slim, attractive, with masses of chestnut brown hair flowing down to the small of her back. On top of her physical appearance, she was smart, kind and funny. What man wouldn't want her?

Amanda left Montague Avenue in a taxi at half one in the morning. Luke and Ireland's World Cup odyssey had come to a sticky end with a 5–2 massacre in the quarter-final against Italy.

As Martina dumped the empty wine bottles into the bin and washed out the wine glasses in the kitchen sink, Luke saw an opportunity to make a point.

'Why don't you go to that place with Amanda?' he said shyly.

Martina turned off the cold tap on the kitchen sink. She looked up at Luke in confusion.

'What place?' she said.

'Erm . . . The Wicked Wolf.'

Martina stared at Luke blankly for a moment, this icy

expression soon melted into a smile. Suddenly Luke felt rather stupid for opening his mouth. It was obvious that his opinion on Martina's love life was irrelevant.

'Night,' she said quietly.

I Hate Dun Laoghaire

Luke sat beneath the shade of Ella's oak tree reading *Everton FC Monthly*, a magazine dedicated to the super toffees. It wasn't a particularly sunny day, but the howling wind had died down from the night before and there was no sign of rain. Luke glanced up from an article about Francis Jeffers, the toffees' teenage striking sensation, to check the time. It was quarter past one, still fifteen minutes of lunch-time left.

'Everton,' a voice said rudely.

Luke looked up, Ella stood in front of him.

'Yeah,' he replied defensively.

Ella stood there, her arms folded across her chest. Luke stared at her, waiting impatiently for a follow-up comment.

'What?' he said bluntly.

'This is my tree,' Ella replied.

Luke smiled. He was about to say, 'don't see your name on it.' At the same time, Ella reached forward and pointed above his head. Luke turned to look. Ella's name was carved in the bark.

'So what?' Luke said in protest.

They stared at one another for a while. It was a stand-off, but something had to give. Luke decided to save grace. He picked up his schoolbag and walked away from the shade of the oak tree.

'Shitty City,' he said quietly, as a parting shot.

Ella took this verbal attack on her beloved Manchester

City in her stride. While bowing her head to study a Ford Mondeo car manual, she held her middle finger aloft to Luke, then used the same digit to press play on her Walkman.

Luke couldn't help but smile at such a classy reply. He shook his head and moved off through the long grass. He walked forward slowly, reading his magazine as he went. As the long grass gave way to the neatly trimmed lawn, Luke looked up at the football pitch. It was deserted, no lunch-time match today. In fact, the only people in the school grounds were Luke, Ella and . . .

'What have we here?'

Luke looked back at the oak tree. Swayne and Casey stood either side of Ella. Swayne snatched her headphones away. Ella casually got to her feet to take them back. Swayne and Casey began a game of piggy in the middle, tossing the head-phones from one to another.

'Come on, nigger, I thought you monkeys could jump really high,' Swayne said loudly.

Ella stood face to face with Swayne. She was on the tips of her toes, her right arm extended high into the air in an attempt to take the headphones back. But Swayne was nearly six foot tall, he kept them out of reach with ease.

'Oa-Oa-Oa,' Swayne said, imitating a monkey.

He looked across at Casey, as a signal. Casey moved forward and took Ella unaware from behind. He locked her arms in a wrestling hold. Casey held Ella steady as Swayne unclipped the Walkman from the front pocket of her dungarees. He held it up in the air for a second, then dropped it to the ground.

'Whoops,' Swayne said softly.

He began stomping his feet on the Walkman, smashing it to pieces. But he wasn't satisfied with the destruction. Swayne scooped the broken carriage off the ground. He removed the cassette and tore the tape apart.

By this time, Luke was already charging back towards the oak tree. He caught Swayne off-guard with a low rugby tackle to the back of his knee joints. Luke pushed hard with all his weight. Swayne crashed headfirst against the tree trunk. Luke wasted no time in following up.

As Swayne collapsed onto the ground in a daze, Luke jumped onto his chest and hammered his right fist against Swayne's nose. It was a great punch, sending a resounding crack into the air.

Luke pulled his fist back to swing again when Casey took hold of his right arm and wrestled him to the ground.

Swayne sat upright against the tree trunk in shock. It took him ten seconds to survey the damage.

'You broke my nose,' he said, with a shriek of pain.

Ella swung her schoolbag against Casey's back and shoulders in an attempt to free Luke from his vice-like clutch. It had little effect. Swayne wiped the puddle of blood dripping from his nostrils and got to his feet. He barged Ella out of the way with a shoulder-charge, knocking her roughly to the ground.

'Little-honchee-bastard,' Swayne said, screaming in anger.

He punctuated each word with a kick to Luke's ribs. The first one cracked him cleanly before Luke wrestled his left arm free of Casey and managed to block and deflect the next three with his arm and elbow. Swayne shoved Casey aside and sat down on top of Luke's chest. He smashed his right fist into Luke's face ten or twelve times. Again, Luke employed his free arm to protect his face from the onslaught. Even so, four powerful punches found their target cleanly.

After watching the clumsy barrage of blows for a whole

minute, even Niall Casey started to feel it was time to show mercy.

'Leave it, Pete, leave it,' he said.

Casey had to use all his strength to pull Swayne away. But he couldn't stop him from booting Luke in the stomach four more times.

'This isn't over, Honchee,' Swayne said.

He fired off one more crisp kick to the ribs. Luke lay on the ground, coughing up a mixture of spit and blood. His face was covered in dark red and purple bruises. He could hardly move his legs or arms. His ribcage felt as though it were on fire. Ella walked across to him. She crouched down beside him and gently moved her hand towards his face.

'Are you OK?' she said.

As her fingers touched his temple, Luke jerked his face away violently. He moved, although it was agony to do so, onto his feet.

'Leave me alone,' he said.

Ella watched as Luke picked up his schoolbag and hobbled through the long grass to the basketball courts. The last thing he wanted to do now was draw more attention to himself. It was becoming clear that Dun Laoghaire hated him. This was fine, Luke hated it back with a passion. Ella stood by the oak tree, watching Luke limp past the other students arriving back for afternoon classes. They all stared at him in confusion as he disappeared out of the school gates onto Woodlawn Drive.

All Alone (Just the way I like it)

Luke had no intention of telling anyone about Swayne's attack. He spent the afternoon at home applying TCP and iodine to his ribs and face. Of course, knowing his luck, this would be the afternoon Martina decided to come home from work early. But thankfully the only thing Luke had to worry about was explaining his Friday afternoon absence to Mr Duffy on Monday morning.

Luke sat by the Packard Bell PC for three hours that afternoon and evening guiding Everton to fourth place in The Premiership and a UEFA Cup Final versus Glasgow Celtic. His injuries were already beginning to heal and he felt a little better. Luke had plenty of time to think about the fight. Swayne's attack was vicious, but Luke had been lucky enough to keep his hands in front of his face during the onslaught. This defence had saved him from more serious damage.

To coincide with his change in mood, a dull grey drizzly afternoon gave way to a gloriously sunny evening. Luke had to be creative with the menu for his dinner. The bare cupboards forced him to improvise with beans on toast. As he sat down to start season 2001/2002 with Everton, the last thing on his mind was going outside. However, six straight defeats in the league forced him to change his mind.

'What?' Luke said in disgust.

The monitor displayed the shocking news that following an emergency board meeting, the directors of Everton FC had terminated Luke Farrell's managerial contract with immediate effect. Luke turned his head to the beams of sunlight splashing onto the kitchen table. It was time for a change of scenery.

'Collins, passes inside to Jeffers,' Luke said.

He was in the middle of the back garden. He side-footed his Mitre leather football against the garden wall. It bounced back to his feet, mimicking a pass from an imaginary teammate.

'Jeffers, drifts pass Stam, cuts inside Berg . . . Goaaal!' Luke said.

He whacked the ball into a gap between the door of the garden shed and the pole for the washing line, or more precisely, the goal-posts at Goodison Park. Luke held his arms aloft and performed a quick lap of honour.

'Everton move into a two-goal lead,' he said.

Luke jogged over to the garden shed. He retrieved the ball and dribbled back to the centre of the garden.

'United kick off, but Hutchinson is in with a super tackle on Keane.'

The fantasy attack moved with a fluid and elegant grace rarely displayed at Goodison Park. Hutchinson knocked it back to Ball. Ball swung it across to Weir. United scampered about in a desperate attempt to cut off the passes. But Weir hit a precise long ball up the line to Barmby. Barmby controlled it, turned and played a neat one-two with Campbell.

'Barmby, skips past Neville. He looks up, knocks it inside.'

He slid the ball against the garden wall. It bounced back and rolled across his path at a steady pace.

'Jeffers,' Luke screamed.

Luke launched his right foot at the ball and connected sweetly. As he followed through with his shot, he slipped on the soggy grass. Luke landed on his arse. He sat on the damp ground watching the ball zoom through the air. It smashed straight through the window of the garden shed.

'Oh no,' Luke said with a groan.

The glass shattered into pieces. Luke could hear the thud of his football whacking against the wall and then bouncing onto the shed floor.

He sat on the damp grass for a second before his brain kicked into gear. No one had witnessed the crime, and if he could just retrieve the evidence, or more precisely his football, no one would be any the wiser. Luke ran towards the garden shed. A few fragments of sharp, jagged glass were all that remained of the window pane.

Luke poked his head through the pane in an attempt to locate his football.

'Woah,' Luke said in amazement.

It was a puzzling sight. The walls of the garden shed were covered with faded yellow pages. Each page had a picture of an old fighter plane from the first and second World Wars. An old-fashioned brown model aeroplane, a fragile construction of cardboard and matchsticky struts, hung from the shed ceiling on a piece of twine like a Christmas tree decoration. It swung back and forth gently, moving in and out of the shaft of sunlight. Luke assumed the football had given it a helpful push before its descent to the floor.

'What are you doing in there?' a voice said firmly.

Luke closed his eyes. Mrs Hendy. Yet again Dun Laoghaire had handed him a bum deal. The old bat would tell Martina, or probably by-pass all that hassle and evict them from her boarding house. Luke turned round to face the music.

'It was an accident,' he said defensively.

Mrs Hendy made brief eye contact with Luke. She walked

forward and glanced through the shattered window pane. Luke couldn't bear the silence. It was all part of the old bat's scheme to make him feel guilty.

'Look, I can replace the window,' Luke said.

Mrs Hendy remained silent. She stood staring at a black and white photograph hanging on the shed wall. Luke followed her gaze.

It was the same as the plane in the photograph. Two bulls-eye targets were painted on the wings. From the flight simulator games on the PC Luke knew it was called a Spitfire. Besides Mr Duffy had pointed it out in a picture book as the plane which won the Battle of Britain.

Mrs Hendy turned back to him with a severe expression. She saw him studying the fighter and something in his expression softened her gaze.

'You know what that plane is?' she said.

'It's a Spitfire, isn't it?'

Mrs Hendy smiled at him. Her face suddenly seemed warm and not a bit severe. But the sadness was still there.

'That's right, a Spitfire.'

She stared at his face and put a practised hand on his shoulder, moving him into the light outside the door.

'What happened to your face?' she said.

Luke gently pressed two fingers against his right cheek.

'I got beaten up,' he replied quietly.

'Bit of beef will cure that,' she said mysteriously. 'Let's get some from the kitchen.'

'I'd rather clean up the shed first,' said Luke.

'Stiff upper lip eh?' said Mrs Hendy, with a smile. But she seemed pleased. Without another word she fetched a brush and dustpan from a small outhouse and sat in an old rocking chair, watching Luke sweep the glass up, dump it in the bin and tidy away the damage done by the football. After a while she seemed to drift off into a world of her own, staring at the picture of the Spitfire.

Luke liked the work. The shed was full of strange stuff. The ball had knocked down a load of old cardboard boxes and Luke noticed an old pair of football boots and a big brown leather football. There was a cardboard box full of ancient comic books called *Chums* and a stack of Biggles books.

'What about this, Mrs Hendy?' said Luke.

He held up a large box which had fallen to the floor from a shelf behind. On the outside it said *Scale Model Kit – Radio Control Included*. There was a picture of a Spitfire taking off from an airstrip on the front cover of the box. A stack of books were piled alongside. *How to Fly R/C, The Beginner's Guide to Model Flight. Constructing your R/C Model.*

Mrs Hendy stared at the box, a little sleepily.

'My, my, I had forgotten about that. Charlie was going to start work on it just before . . .'

She stopped. She swallowed. She took off her spectacles and got up stiffly. She looked at Luke.

'Is your mother home?'

Luke was nervous about answering no. But if he lied and Mrs Hendy called his bluff, things would be a lot worse.

'No. She has night college Monday to Thursday,' Luke said quietly.

'What time does she get home?'

'After eleven.'

'Would you like tea and cake?' Mrs Hendy said.

Luke was gob-smacked. The one person he was certain would come down on him like a ton of bricks was inviting him in for tea and cake. Mrs Hendy turned round from the shed door. Luke had no voice to answer yes. Instead, he nodded his head in agreement. He followed Mrs Hendy across the damp lawn to the back door. He would still get hell from Martina about breaking the window.

Luke sat on the couch in the back sitting room, holding a piece of beef to his cheek. The door swung open gently, Mrs Hendy pushed a small serving trolley in front of Luke. A two-storey silver platter was stuffed full of cakes. Chocolate éclairs, jam and cream doughnuts, coffee slices. Steam piped from the spout of a stately silver teapot.

'Look after yourself, Luke,' Mrs Hendy said.

She had used his name. Maybe she wouldn't tell Martina after all. Luke dumped the beef and reached for an éclair. Mrs Hendy smiled as he stuffed his face. They turned, almost conspiratorially as a knock sounded on the door.

'All done, Mrs Hendy,' a muffled male voice said from outside the parlour door.

'That's the fellow who fixed the window,' Mrs Hendy said to Luke with a wink. She picked up her purse. 'Excuse me.'

She went out to pay the gruff voice. Luke moved to the piano and studied the old photograph. No doubt about it. The young woman was Mrs Hendy.

'Good as new. No need to tell your mother,' Mrs Hendy said behind him. He felt that she might have been watching him for a few seconds before she spoke. She picked up the photograph and smiled sadly at Luke.

'You're wondering why he looks like me?'

Luke nodded. She was no fool.

'That's my brother Charlie.' She seemed to draw a deep breath. Her voice shook a little. 'The other boy's Jimmy Hendy, his best friend.'

She looked at Luke and seemed to make up her mind about something. She stared at the picture with misty eyes.

'Jimmy and I were engaged to be married.'

Luke tried to say something adult – and walked into it.

'Did you break it off?'

Mrs Hendy put her hand on the piano for a moment. As if she would fall if she didn't. She spoke softly, as if in pain.

'He was killed in the Battle of Britain. The fifth of September 1940.'

Luke didn't know what to do or say. Mrs Hendy seemed so small just then. But after a moment she straightened her back, smiled brightly at Luke and opened the little box. She took out the medal and let Luke hold it in his hand.

'They gave him this for bravery.'

Luke stared at it. For bravery.

'Would you like to hear the whole story?' she said.

Luke nodded hard. He wanted to hear the whole story. And he knew somehow that Mrs Hendy wanted to tell it.

Mrs Hendy sat by the fire, and as the light died outside, and Luke climbed the mountain of cake, she took them back to that hot heroic summer of 1940 when she was in her last year at school and called Sarah Kingston. By the time she had finished, Luke had forgotten to eat, but sat there with a melting éclair in his hand.

The house on Montague Avenue had been in her family for three generations. Her father was a bank clerk and her mother a music teacher. They were part of the old professional Protestant class, proud to be Irish. But after 1922, when Ireland gained its independence, they sometimes felt like foreigners.

Tell me about it, thought Luke. Like being a northsider on the southside.

Growing up, she and her brother Charlie had known few people outside the small Church of Ireland community. Catholics and Protestants didn't mix much back before the Second World War. The Catholic Church was anxious to cut down contact for fear of what they called 'mixed marriages'.

But then she had met Jimmy Hendy. Jimmy was a Catholic but he was Charlie's best friend. The friendship had been forged playing soccer for Rock Rovers. Luke stared at her.

'What position?' he said automatically.

Mrs Hendy did not hesitate.

'Jimmy was a centre forward, Charlie was a winger.'

Luke looked at her with new respect. Apart from saying soccer instead of football, Mrs Hendy was definitely on the ball.

'Jimmy was a joy. He had black hair and blue eyes, and a laugh that would lift the saddest heart, and, of course, I fell in love with him.'

Luke leaned in. Of late the word love had taken on a new interest. He felt that Mrs Hendy would neither mock nor laugh if he told her some of the things he thought from time to time.

'How old were you?' he asked carefully.

Mrs Hendy smiled at him.

'Not much older than you.' She smiled again, and her eyes softened. 'Sweet seventeen and never been kissed.' She paused. 'Until Jimmy kissed me.'

Charlie and his girlfriend, Beatrice, covered for them so they could meet in secret. Both families would have been angry at the breach of religious apartheid. In fact all four of them wanted to marry but, for different reasons, could not do so – Jimmy and Sarah because of religion, and Charles and Beatrice because neither had a good job.

'It might never have happened but for Hitler,' said Mrs Hendy.

Luke looked at her in surprise. Mrs Hendy smiled.

'As soon as the war broke out the four of us packed our bags and took the mailboat to England,' Mrs Hendy said. 'Jimmy and I were married in a registry office with Charlie as best man and Beatrice as bridesmaid. Then we were best man and bridesmaid for Charlie and Beatrice. We had our honeymoon in London.'

Luke stared at Mrs Hendy's face. Somehow the years had rolled away and she was smiling like a girl.

'The Luftwafe dropped bombs all night. Jimmy said he never heard a thing. He said all he could hear was my heart.'

Mrs Hendy fell silent. She looked at the fire for a while. ·

'Next morning Jimmy and Charlie joined the RAF,' she said flatly. 'Beatrice had been brought up by the sea so we joined the WRENS.' She caught Luke's lost look. 'Women's Royal Navy Service. We nursed the wounded from the warships.'

No wonder she knew about beef for bruises, Luke thought. He stared at her. Noticed the steel in her eyes. Hitler took on the wrong woman when he took on Mrs Hendy.

She passed the picture across to Luke. 'That's the four of us, somewhere in Sussex.' Luke looked up at the strange phrase. Mrs Hendy smiled. 'Security. You always said "somewhere in Sussex".'

Luke looked at the four laughing figures in the frame, the Spitfire, and for the first time he noticed what looked like patches on the fuselage. He put his finger on it. Mrs Hendy took a long, long breath.

'It was the fifth of September, 1940.' Mrs Hendy knew it by heart. 'Jimmy and Charlie were flying Spitfire Mk IIs over Beachy Head in East Sussex. Charlie said it reminded him of Howth. They were waiting for Heinkel one eleven bombers.'

Mrs Hendy stared fiercely into the past as she reeled off the names. And suddenly Luke realised with a shock that she had been in a real war, been under the bombers, seen dead bodies. She knew all the military names as well as she knew the names of her neighbours' cats.

'The Heinkels flew in a tight formation. They clustered together so they could fire in any direction, moving like a pack of wolves.'

Luke nodded. Like a Christmas tree formation in football.

'The Spitfires had to cut their way into the centre. And then pick them off one by one. Jimmy liked doing that.' She looked away. 'Jimmy always liked to carry the fight to the enemy.'

Of course he did, thought Luke. Jimmy was a centre forward. What else would he do?

Mrs Hendy got up and poked the fire; her back to Luke, her voice muffled by the poking, and the roar of flames.

'That day the Heinkels gave the Acklington lads a terrible time. Charlie had been downed in a dogfight, he had to bale out. He got down safely and stood in a ploughed field. Jimmy was on his own. And the second wave of Heinkels were coming in on their way to London.'

Mrs Hendy smiled briefly. 'Jimmy used to say the Heinkels had spoiled his honeymoon. And that he would give them a good hammering every time he met them.'

Mrs Hendy stopped. And Luke knew she was seeing fluffy white clouds, a blue sky, the green water of the English Channel below, and that lonely little wasp heading out to meet the swarm of bluebottles.

'Charlie said that Jimmy flew over him and dipped his wings before turning out to sea where the Heinkels were. He watched him all the way. The last thing he saw was a Spitfire flying into the sun.'

Mrs Hendy was silent for a long time. So was Luke.

Something was stuck in his throat, and his eyes felt itchy. But there was something that he had to ask.

'Mrs Hendy, why is the model Spitfire still in its box?'

Mrs Hendy turned and looked at him sadly. 'The Spitfire in the shed. That's another story.'

Mrs Hendy sat down heavily. She told him what happened after the war. Mrs Hendy had come home a widow. Her parents died shortly after. Charles and Beatrice had come to live with her in the big old house. She never married again.

'Jimmy was my true love,' she said simply. 'What we had was perfect and so I was happy to hold him in my memory.'

'And the Spitfire?' Luke prompted

Mrs Hendy smiled forgivingly.

'Charlie was very cast down. First Jimmy and, later, Beatrice. He spent more and more time in the shed, turning over the old planes, reading the old comics, trying to hold the happy memories when he and Jimmy were on top of the world.'

Mrs Hendy bit her lip before she went on.

'One Christmas I thought I would cheer Charlie up with a surprise. I had seen an advert for a model Spitfire in a magazine. So I sent away for it. Charlie said he would fly it over the Hill of Howth for me. In memory of Jimmy.'

Mrs Hendy looked away again.

'Charlie died before he could even open the box. We didn't even start to build the damn thing. After he died I had to take lodgers. The British army give me a pension but this is a big old house.'

Mrs Hendy sighed and fell silent.

Luke wasn't listening. He had an idea about the Spitfire. And when Luke had an idea he liked to get down to it immediately. He stood up suddenly.

'Erm . . . I'd better go,' Luke said.

The sound of his voice seemed to snap Mrs Hendy out of her trance. She got to her feet and touched his cheek in goodbye.

'Thanks for the tea and cake,' Luke said.

Mrs Hendy smiled.

'Thank you for the tea and sympathy.'

She held the door open for him. She gave him a nod. She shut the door. He thought he heard a sob but couldn't be sure.

When he reached the top of the first staircase he stared down to where the garden shed was shrouded in shadow. Part of his brain argued that his idea was intrusive and rude. But it was only part. The rest of his brain said go for goal. There was only one way to find out. Do it. Dither never beat a defender.

Luke was sitting at the table by the window, doodling red, white and blue bullseyes on a magazine, thinking about the Spitfire idea – because that was what it was – when he heard voices on the landing. A key turned in the lock. He heard his mother's bright voice. Far too bright for a woman after a hard day's work.

'This is Ronald,' Martina said. 'Ronald, this is Luke.'

Martina was standing beside a smiley stranger with a big hairy moustache. Luke looked at him with loathing.

'Hello,' Ronald said softly, waving his hand to accompany his friendly smile. There was something strange about his voice, as if he was pronouncing his words carefully. Luke wondered was he drunk. His father, Jay, used to speak that way when he was pissed.

'Ronald's from Holland,' Martina said helpfully. She moved into the kitchen. 'You never touched your pizza.'

Luke let himself look starved, and hoped she'd never find out about Mrs Hendy's hill of cakes.

'I loff pizza,' said Ronald.

Luke stared at Ronald with an expression of pure hatred. He didn't quite understand the emotion, but Luke sensed an immediate danger from Ronald's presence in their lives. Martina stared at Luke and tensed up.

'Luke, say hello,' she said.

Luke allowed six long seconds slouch by before coldly replying, 'Hello,' in a clean, crisp voice. Ronald nodded his head happily. He knew he was under rigorous observation.

So did Martina. She fluttered about the kitchen, retrieving cans of Coke from the fridge, talking in an unusually bright and breezy voice. Luke touched the receding bruise on his right cheek. Martina was so wrapped up in the visit of this hairy monster she didn't bother to notice his injuries.

Luke picked up a school book – but of course this was only a cover so he could covertly watch the couple.

Ronald took a seat by the Packard Bell PC. Martina sat beside him with plates of food. Ronald cleaned his plate and made cool computer moves at the same time. He was a good teacher and Martina made good progress. So did Ron with Martina.

'Very clever,' Luke said to himself.

It seemed Ronald was a tutor in Programming and Operating Systems at Dun Laoghaire college. He had been 'kind enough' to offer Martina some 'extra' tuition.

'Very, very clever,' Luke said silently.

For the next forty minutes, Martina sat by Ronald's side as he showed her the principles of changing the Settings on Windows 95. Luke hovered about in the background, sipping a bottle of Lucozade Sport. Ronald had moved the lesson onto setting up a basic workbook in Microsoft Excel when Martina made a suggestion.

'Luke, it's after twelve,' she said.

Martina gave her order, humiliating Luke in front of the Dutch geek, without even looking his way. This just wouldn't do.

'So?'

Martina turned to face Luke in an instant.

'Excuse me?' she said.

It was a stand-off. Ronald continued to click the mouse, pretending to be deeply interested in Workbook 1 on Microsoft Excel. Luke concentrated his stare on the back of Ronald's neck. It was dripping with sweat. He was obviously feeling the tension. Luke found courage, this wasn't the time to back down, or in essence, go to bed.

'You've never told me to go to bed before,' Luke said innocently.

It was an outstanding argument, with all the brilliance of a swerving Roberto Carlos free-kick. Martina was fuming, Ronald was sweating buckets. Luke stood his ground, arms folded, awaiting her reply.

'Well, I'm telling you now. Go to bed.'

Luke allowed his jaw to drop in disbelief, followed by ten seconds of tension-soaked silence. He let his deep green eyes droop sadly, walked over to the couch and gathered together his Geography text book. With his head bowed, Luke marched across the living room slowly. He quietly closed his bedroom door.

'Game, set and match,' Luke said, whispering to himself.

Martina would be sitting at the Packard Bell PC, her heart torn into little pieces of guilt, shame and regret. Ronald would be asked to pack away his notepad, stick his leather satchel beneath his left arm and leave their lives, forever.

Luke lay on his bed, waiting for the muffled sounds to signal his victory. The first thing he heard was Martina talking. Good, this was her explanation to Ronald, asking him to understand. Now Ronald was talking; even better, he was mumbling about his upset. Now Martina would erect a dignified wall of silence and the Dutch geek would be on his way.

However, the next sound was a little unexpected. Luke strained forward to be certain. Laughter, surely not. But it wasn't a 'Sorry things didn't work out' kind of laughter. This was more a 'Sorry about my immature child' hilarity. Luke sat up, straining harder to make out the sounds. It seemed his confident attitude was a mistake. Martina 1 Luke 0.

Luke seethed for a while. But then decided he could salvage something from the night by starting Operation Spitfire. He rolled over and set his alarm for three hours ahead. Ronald would be long gone by three a.m. Synchronise your watches. He fell asleep, fully dressed, ready for action.

Luke sat up in bed. The only thing he could make out in the darkness was the red digits on his Sanyo electronic alarm clock. They showed three am. Luke slipped his runners on over his bare feet and tiptoed past the closed door of the living room. He stopped in shock. Light shone under the door. Music came softly. He heard Martina laugh like a cat force-fed a carton of cream.

Luke closed the front door behind him gently and ghosted down the staircase. He stood inside the kitchen, reaching out his hands aimlessly in the darkness. Suddenly, he had an award-winning idea to throw some light on the situation. Luke opened the fridge door, illuminating the greater part of the kitchen. To the left of the gas oven, a key rack hung on the wall.

As Luke moved across the damp lawn, his runners squelched with each soggy step forward. A dog barked in a nearby garden, it seemed to have a domino effect. Suddenly four different barks echoed out across the neighbourhood.

Luke froze on the spot, illuminated by the razor sharp beams of moonlight. He shuffled across to the cover of the garden wall. Luke felt safe in the shade and made speedy progress round the perimeter of the back garden to the door of the shed.

Although he was fifty feet away from the house, Luke took great care not to jangle the keys. He took his time, patiently trying each one in the padlock. Finally, he found the right one.

The shed door creaked open, its hinges aching for oil. Luke went inside, leaving the door ajar. He picked up the model kit, tucking it beneath his left armpit. Just as he turned to leave, Luke had a brainwave.

'Oh yeah,' he said in a hushed whisper.

Luke bent down onto one knee. He could barely make out the writing in the darkness, so he went for a lucky dip. He plucked a book from the top of the pile, got to his feet and walked out of the shed.

Before padlocking the shed door, Luke placed the model kit and book on the damp concrete path outside. He pulled the shed door shut and locked up. Then he lifted the book into the moonlight to read the title. *How to Fly R/C*. Bingo. Luke made his way back to the house under the shadow of the garden wall. He was smiling, confident that his theft would bring happiness.

Back in his room, Luke spent at least twenty minutes carefully unpacking the Spitfire parts. They didn't look like much all separated. Maybe the book would help him make sense of them but he didn't think so. Luke was not mechanically minded.

His gloomy thoughts were interrupted by noises from the living room. He heard the door to the landing close and two people clump down the stairs. Luke shot swiftly into the now vacant living room and pulled back the curtain to watch the action below.

Ronald came down the concrete steps. He waved his shovel-sized hand back at the front door, then ate up the pavement with his long lanky strides. Luke heard the front door creak, then lock. He raced back into his bedroom before Martina came back.

Luke climbed beneath his duvet, but he had no intention of sleeping. There was a strong possibility that Ronald and his mother had shared a kiss. The process of goodbye had expanded from, 'I'll show you to the front door', to a lengthy five minute stall between their exit from the living room and his appearance outside. The uncertainty was killing Luke. He just had to know.

Martina was closing down Windows 95 on the PC when Luke walked across to the kitchen sink. He blindly filled a glass with water, centring his attention on Martina. Luke felt sure he could tell without asking a question. She was smiling, gently wrapping a lock of her long brown hair round her index finger.

'Night,' Martina said.

Luke watched her float into her bedroom. It was a fact. Ronald was Martina's boyfriend. His suspicions were correct.

Luke gave a theatrical groan.

GETTING OFF THE GROUND

Woodlawn Comprehensive had certain advantages to offer Luke and Operation Spitfire. Not least was a good workshop.

'Where's part g-27?' Luke said quietly.

Mr Ambrose, the metalwork teacher, had left for lunch five minutes ago. Luke was all alone now in metalwork room one, standing with the main construction schematic spread across his desk. The operation to construct the Spitfire had run into . . . 'a few minor difficulties'. The main problem being, Luke had no idea what he was doing.

'What?' Luke said in high-pitched astonishment.

He scratched his forehead with the butt of his H2 pencil. The assembly instructions said he should join part g-27 with b-449.

'What is b-449?' Luke asked.

He looked about the deserted metalwork room, realising he had started talking to himself. He slumped down onto his stool and dumped his H2 pencil onto the schematic. It rolled back and forth along the curled-up edge of the smooth blue paper three or four times before coming to a halt.

Luke had been working on the Spitfire for three whole weeks and not even one wing was assembled. All he had to show for his efforts were a mountain of paper-cuts on the tips of his fingers and an expensive bill for tubes of Loctite Superglue 3.

'Balls to this,' Luke said quietly.

He took the H2 pencil, placed it behind his left ear, rolled up the construction schematic and tied it with an elastic band. Luke carefully placed the components of the Spitfire back into the rectangular box. He worked in silence until his concentration was broken by the rev of a car engine. Luke closed the lid of the box, dumped the *How to Fly R/C* book on top, and went off to investigate the sound.

It was coming from inside metalwork room two. Luke tip-toed across the hall and creaked open the door of metalwork room two slightly. On the far side of the room, the yard doors were swung wide open. Mr Duffy was leaning against the control panel of a lathe, watching someone working beneath the bonnet of his green Toyota Corolla.

'Try it now, sir,' a female voice said.

Mr Duffy stood up from the control panel and got into the drivers seat. The mystery mechanic came up from the depths of the engine and wiped her hands with a paper towel. It was Ella Barnes, covered in oil, decked out in dirty grey overalls.

Mr Duffy started the Corolla's engine. It hummed like a bumble bee heading back to the hive with a sack full of pollen. Mr Duffy smiled and stuck his lofted thumb out of the side window. Luke pulled the door shut before he was noticed.

Luke tapped on Mrs Hendy's door. Tea and cakes on a Thursday had become a regular ritual. Both of them looked forward to it more than either would admit.

'Oh, hello,' Mrs Hendy said.

Luke held out his left hand. Mrs Hendy took the plastic bag from him and walked into the kitchen.

'How was school?' she said.

'OK,' Luke replied.

He stood by the kitchen table as Mrs Hendy unloaded the

groceries into the fridge. Luke wanted to tell her about his problems assembling the Spitfire. It seemed like the kind of thing Mrs Hendy would love to hear about. But he couldn't, after all, it wouldn't be much of a surprise then. But he told her other things.

Mrs Hendy closed the fridge door. She opened the freezer door, letting a puffy cloud of icy vapour escape. She started to pack away frozen peas, chips and beef burgers. Mrs Hendy looked across at Luke, smiling.

'How's your little friend?' she said.

Mrs Hendy was referring to Cecilia. Luke had started to struggle for topics of conversation to occupy the time in his visits to the back parlour for tea and cake. The tale of Rathdale Athletic's glorious stride towards a historic league and cup double took a mere half hour to recount. Since then, tales of life with Martina in Rathdale, and eventually the goings on in Woodlawn Comprehensive, had come into play.

'I haven't spoken to her in ages,' Luke said.

'Why not?' Mrs Hendy replied.

She handed Luke a Choc-Ice from the freezer as an incentive for some juicy gossip. Luke removed the wrapper, took a bite, shrugged his shoulder and said, 'Just haven't.'

Mrs Hendy watched Luke walk off towards the kitchen door. He stepped out onto the lawn for a quick kickabout before tea. After that, it was back to the drawing board with the Spitfire.

'Arggh,' Luke said, screaming in anger.

'Stupid, fu . . .'

He looked across at the swear jar on top of the fridge. He was deeply tempted to load it up with three weeks' worth of pocket money, just so he could tell the Spitfire *exactly* how he felt. Part h-1101 was stuck to Luke's left elbow.

'Arggh,' he said, crying in pain as he peeled it away. Shredded pieces of skin separated onto their new home of part h-1101.

Assembling the Spitfire really was a blood, sweat and tears job. At that precise moment, Luke's forehead was drenched in sweat. His left elbow was bleeding and tears of pain, anger and madness streamed down his cheeks.

Luke had spent the last five hours working on the left wing. He looked at the mangled mass of screws, nuts and wooden beams and wondered what he had actually done.

Nothing.

Luke didn't want to admit it. But building things wasn't exactly his expertise. After wrapping his elbow in a bandage of Kitten Soft quilted toilet paper, he packed away the parts and called it a night. He had other things to worry about besides Operation Spitfire. Well, one thing really. Ronald Van De Kieft.

BACK IN THE FRYING PAN

Luke couldn't concentrate. He was sitting against the trunk of Ella's oak tree, holding the Spitfire assembly instructions in front of his face. Morning break was five minutes old and the sun had taken an opportunity to shine for the first time in weeks.

The only image in his mind was that of Ronald Van De Kieft. A six foot seven computer programmer from Amsterdam with long bushy brown hair, a moustache, and tragic taste in clothing.

As if his moss-green corduroy trousers and black leather slip-on shoes weren't bad enough. He wore a lemon silk shirt. He was, without any shadow of a doubt, a prat.

When Luke had suggested to Martina that she go out and look for a boyfriend, he'd been thinking more along the lines of a wealthy businessman. Ronald didn't look wealthy; weird maybe, but not wealthy.

'Hi,' a voice said.

Luke snapped out of his daze. Cecilia was standing in front of him, smiling. Before he could reply, she sat down beside him. There was nothing he could do now. The entire student population of Woodlawn had watched her walk fifty yards across the grounds to sit beside him. Luke spotted Swayne and Co by the bike shed. Swayne's expression was far from a happy one.

'What are you reading?' Cecilia asked.

Luke looked back at Cecilia. He folded the assembly instructions in half and handed them to her. She looked at them blankly as he explained.

'My landlady. Her fiancé was a fighter pilot in World War Two. He was killed in the Battle of Britain. I thought I'd bring her out to Howth Head and fly this model Spitfire to honour his memory.'

Cecilia wore a blank smile. She didn't seem interested in a single word Luke said. In fact, it didn't seem like she was listening at all.

'You don't wave to me anymore,' she said softly.

'No,' Luke replied blankly.

He was busy keeping an eye on Swayne.

'Why not?'

Cecilia awaited an answer. Luke was lost for words. He abandoned three possible replies as stupid. But refusing to answer, to remain completely silent would be rude. He needed to say something. In the end, he went for the truth.

'I'm not sure what to say to you,' he said shyly.

Cecilia moved her gaze from the ground, straight into Luke's eyes, then back to the ground again. Her stare was like a blinding ray of sunlight burning into his eyeballs. Luke tried to breathe normally. But her sheer presence made him nervous. She picked a fallen twig up from the grass and scratched a little love-heart in the dirt between them, complete with Cupid's arrow.

'Just say hello,' Cecilia said softly.

Luke felt her press her left hand against the inside of his thigh, using it as leverage as she got to her feet. He watched her saunter through the long grass towards the basketball courts. The love-heart was still intact on the ground. The message was clear. Although he tried desperately, Luke couldn't bring himself to scratch away her symbol of affection.

Mr O'Shea appeared on the basketball courts, ringing his trusty brass bell. Luke was so overwhelmed by Cecilia's visit that he walked off towards the main building, leaving the assembly instructions by the oak tree.

It was only when fierce pellets of rain started to crash against the window of room nineteen that Luke remembered the assembly instructions. He threw his left hand high into the air, catching Miss Court's attention.

'Yes,' she said wearily.

'Can I go the toilet, Miss?' Luke replied.

Miss Court seemed troubled by his request. Luke expected a pointless rendition of the old teacher classic of, 'Can't you wait till lunch-time?' or 'Why didn't you go before the class started?'

'Oh, go on,' she said with a sigh.

Luke grabbed his rainjacket and headed for the door.

'Mr Farrell,' Miss Court said.

Luke stopped dead. He turned round to face the attentive eyes of Miss Court and his 2C classmates.

'Do you really need your jacket in the toilets?' she said.

Luke stood there, silent. He made no attempt to answer, but Miss Court had no intention of letting him off the hook so easily this time. He decided to cut his losses and threw his jacket beneath the desk.

By the time he reached the oak tree the rain had eased off slightly. Luckily, the instructions had been covered by a thick branch hanging directly overhead. Luke stuffed them beneath his jumper and sprinted back towards the main building.

As he reached the main door, the bell for the end of morning classes rang out. Luke walked along the deserted main corridor. Suddenly he found himself battling through a tide of bodies rushing in the opposite direction. It was like swimming up Niagara Falls.

When he finally reached room nineteen, Miss Court stood outside, waiting impatiently.

'Impeccable timing, Mr Farrell,' she said sarcastically.

Luke ignored this remark. He went straight inside room nineteen and retrieved his schoolbag and rainjacket from beneath the desk.

'Thanks, Miss,' he said quietly.

He departed room nineteen, passing by Miss Court who stood outside waiting to lock the door. Luke pulled his rain-jacket over his head then slung his schoolbag over his shoulder, all the while walking down the corridor. He was on his way to metalwork room one.

'Honchee,' Swayne said.

Luke noticed Swayne standing in the corridor behind him. Straight away he knew it was about Cecilia. Luke had no great desire to enter into a discussion, but the sight of Casey and Co blocking his path up ahead changed his opinion on things.

Luke stood between the two electric hand-dryers on the wall opposite the urinals. Casey kept a look-out at the main toilet door while Swayne paced up and down the floor in front of him like a seasoned homicide detective waiting to start an interrogation.

The discussion about Cecilia was yet to begin. But Luke could read Swayne's mind like a *Mr Men* book. This silent delay was a crude tactic to make him sweat.

'Come on, I haven't got all day,' Luke said impatiently.

Swayne's measured pacing came to an abrupt halt. He turned, rushed forward in a flash and grasped a handful of Everton jersey.

'I've warned you, Honchee,' Swayne said.

'What?' Luke replied.

'Stay clear of Cecilia.'

It was a fair warning. But how could Luke reply? If he pointed out the truth, that Cecilia fancied him and had made all the running, it was time for another knuckle sandwich. But if Luke caved in and stayed clear, he would be giving in to a bully.

On top of all that, he would *certainly* blow his chance with Cecilia. It was time to stand firm. 'Do you fancy her?' Luke thought to himself. 'Don't ask stupid questions' he replied. 'Then stand up for yourself !!!' That was that, time to listen to your heart, time to be a man.

'You can't make me stay away from her,' he said firmly.

Swayne raised his upper lip to form a sinister sneer.

'Can't I?' he replied softly.

Luke took his beating like a man. Swayne and Co left the 5th year toilets safe in the knowledge he understood the message. But they were gravely mistaken. With blood pouring from both nostrils and his ribs and arms aching with a fiery pain, Luke walked out of the toilets.

He came out the main school entrance in time to see Swayne and Co mounting their bikes in the bike shed. He watched them ride out of the school gates onto Woodlawn Drive like a posse of outlaws in the Wild West. The only people left in the school grounds were leaning under the bonnet of a silver Ford Capri in the car park.

'Do you have the manual, sir?' Ella said.

Her question seemed to snap Mr Ambrose out of a day-dream. He stood up straight.

'The manual, of course. I'll be back in a minute,' he replied.

As he made his way back across the car park to the teachers' entrance, Ella popped her head up and placed her hands against the small of her back and stretched backwards. It was only when she began rotating her aching shoulders to breathe some life back into her body that she spotted Luke. He was a good distance away, but it was clear he had taken a beating.

Luke noticed Ella staring across. He glanced back at her momentarily before making his way to the edge of the football pitch. Although he paid no attention to her, Ella watched Luke closely. He began stretching his hamstrings, calves and groin. He removed his tracksuit bottoms and placed them in his schoolbag.

'Thanks,' Ella said as Mr Ambrose handed her the manual.

He joined her in watching Luke, who performed short sprints along the touchline of the football pitch.

'He's keen,' Mr Ambrose said.

'Yeah,' Ella replied blankly.

'Perhaps your dad should sign him up for the Enders,' Mr Ambrose said with a smile.

Ella nodded her head in silent agreement.

Over by the football pitch, Luke sat down behind a goalpost and ate his lunch. Afterwards he sipped half his bottle of Lucozade Sport in preparation. He was about to make a stand against Swayne and Co, the best way he knew how.

The players involved in the daily lunch-time game arrived back in Woodlawn Comprehensive at one o'clock. They stared at Luke in confusion, whispering to each other about his sudden desire to play football. Luke ignored the gossip. He continued his warm-up exercises.

Swayne and Co were the last to arrive. When they did, the

sight of Luke togged out for football was almost too good to be true.

'Thank you, God,' Swayne said, drawing smirks and giggles from every member of Co.

When Ella finished the tune-up of Mr Ambrose's car, she walked across to the touchline of the football pitch. She was waiting for her father, Jerome, to arrive. They had arranged to meet in the teachers' car park for quarter past one. They were going to a second-hand car auction in Sallynoggin that afternoon.

Meanwhile, Cecilia and her gang had caught wind of Luke's participation in the daily football match. In fact, this revelation had caused a frenzy of excitement to run through the students of 2C. Only Tonka Matthews abstained from the football fever. He chose instead to lean against a basketball pole, reading *Kerrang* magazine while listening to Megadeath on his Walkman.

Swayne and Co took the red bibs. Luke waited for them to do this before going across to join the blues. His team was made up of 1st years and a couple of faces from 2C.

'Right. We'll play 4–4–2,' Alan Giles said

He was the blue goalkeeper and Cecilia's twin brother. Natural blonde, but not quite as beautiful. He shared her clear complexion and even features but carried the odd excess pound around the midriff.

'What position do you play, Luke?' Alan said.

The blues looked at their new team-mate in curiosity.

'Up front or right midfield,' Luke replied.

Alan nodded his head, he looked about the other players. As self-appointed manager, it was up to Alan to reshuffle the line-up to fit Luke in.

'Copper, you play centre-midfield. Dave, drop to right-back,' Alan said.

Two players nodded their heads. One was a small kid wearing an Arsenal jersey. He had dark red hair and a face full of freckles. The other was a tall, rake-thin 1st year wearing a yellow Liverpool jersey. He had jet-black hair, long gangly legs and vaguely familiar features.

Luke stared at the kid for a while longer before it hit him.

'Is your name Swayne?' Luke asked bluntly.

The kid was stunned by the question. He remained silent but nodded his head. Luke sighed in disgust. Perfect, not only did he have to worry about Swayne and Co trying to chop him in two every time he touched the ball, he also had Swayne Junior to stab him in the back.

The blue team lined out on the pitch. They waited for the reds to kick-off.

'Alright, babe,' a deep voice said.

Ella felt her father's fingertips on her shoulders. Jerome had obviously been for a jog. He was wearing his black Adidas tracksuit and his Man Utd bobble hat. His attention quickly centred on the football match.

'Hey, all you Enders. Game on Saturday, no crunchers,' he said, shouting in a broad Manchester accent.

Jerome's remark caught the attention of every player on the pitch. Luke glanced over at the touchline. He concentrated on Ella, standing beside Jerome. He was a man mountain. Well over six foot tall and built like a black Sherman tank.

Luke noticed Cecilia standing on the touchline, five feet to the left of Ella. She smiled and gave him a little wave. Luke turned to face Swayne, who had been paying close attention to Cecilia's provocative gesture. He wore a furious snarl. Talk about waving a red flag in front of a bull.

The reds kicked off. Casey knocked the ball back to Swayne. He and Luke locked stares. It was time to play football.

Swayne charged forward, Luke ran to tackle him. This was a make or break challenge, quite literally. Swayne let the ball run a few feet ahead of him. As Luke moved in to intercept, Swayne slid, two-footed, to block.

'Woah, easy,' Jerome shouted.

The force of Swayne's sliding tackle knocked Luke into the air. It was a clear free-kick to the blues. Despite a heavy fall, Luke got to his feet and dusted himself down without any fuss. Swayne stood right in front of the ball.

'Yards,' Luke said firmly.

Swayne reluctantly backed off ten yards. Luke looked about the pitch. The reds were out of position. He took advantage of their defensive blunder and chipped the ball over the top, catching the defence cold.

Copper was alive to the chance. He ghosted onto Luke's long ball and hit a low shot to the keeper's right. Unfortunately the keeper got down well and turned the ball round the post for a corner.

'Good ball,' Jerome said, clapping his hands together.

Cecilia edged her gang closer to Ella and Jerome to hear his expert judgement on Luke's performance.

'Come on, Luke,' she said loudly.

Ella shot Cecilia a quick glance, tutting quietly to herself. 'What does she know about football?' David Swayne jogged across to take the corner kick. Luke stood on the edge of the six-yard box, closely marked by Casey and Swayne.

'Yeah,' Luke shouted. He made a sudden sprint across the penalty area. David Swayne heard his call and knocked the ball towards his feet. Luke took a split-second glance over his right shoulder. Casey was rushing towards him like a freight train.

As Casey dived in with a clumsy sliding tackle designed to injure, Luke dummied the ball and spun past him. Swayne came charging out to block the shot, but Luke had enough time to smash the ball low into the bottom corner, beating the keeper on his near post.

'Good goal,' Jerome said, clapping his hands enthusiastically.

Cecilia let out a piercing squeal of delight. She clapped her hands together and whooped in celebration. No one else on the touchline bothered to join her. But after a quick glance in her direction, her stagnant friends offered Luke a belated round of applause.

Swayne and Casey had already started to argue amongst themselves about the goal, laying the blame at each other's door. Luke received the congratulations of his team-mates. But he made a special effort to salute David Swayne with a thumbs up.

'Ella,' Jerome said quietly.

Ella looked up at her father, whose attention was centred on the red team kicking off.

'Who's that kid in blue?'

Swayne and Co had four minutes left to salvage some pride or seriously injure Luke. So far, they had managed neither. A steadily growing crowd on the touchline cheered every time Luke got the ball. It was 3–0 to the blues; a hat-trick of astounding quality from Luke. Jerome stood on the touchline, watching in disbelief.

'That kid's got everything,' he said in wonder.

Cecilia overheard Jerome's comment. It fastened a smug smile to her lips. Luke was a sporting hero, exactly the kind of boyfriend she desired. It was all before her, winner of *Star Search 2000*, record contract, chart success, fame, stardom, four page spread in *Hello*. And now, the icing on the cake, a famous footballing boyfriend.

She clapped in encouragement.

'Come on, Luke,' Cecilia said, elevating her voice above the crowd.

Ella pinned a spiteful stare in her direction. She stopped paying attention to the action on the football pitch. Cecilia soon became aware that Ella was staring at her. It felt like a magnifying glass burning a ray of sunlight onto the side of her temple.

At first she tried to shrug it off with a friendly smile. But Ella continued to stare. Cecilia became concerned.

'What?' she asked nervously.

'He's good, isn't he?' Ella said.

Cecilia nodded her head, wearing her pearly white smile as a reply. But Ella wasn't passing a polite comment. She was curious to discuss Luke's performance.

'But do you think he's playing a little too deep?'

Cecilia defended her complete ignorance concerning all matters football with her trusty sweetheart smile and a well timed, non-committal reply.

'I suppose so.'

Ella held a piercing scream in her throat. She felt like vomiting onto the pitch, or punching Cecilia in her pretty little face.

'You're dead, Honchee,' Swayne said, in between his laboured gasps for air.

Luke smiled. They were standing together on the halfway line. But while Luke stood on his toes, waiting for Alan's kick out, Swayne was bent over, hands on knees, trying to suck in some oxygen.

Luke had dragged him all over the pitch, making him look stupid through sheer footballing brilliance on nine or ten separate occasions. His second goal was a cheeky glancing header at the near post from a pinpoint David Swayne corner, while his third was a power-bolt free-kick through the wall from the edge of the penalty-area.

Co were also feeling the pace after chasing Luke around the pitch for twenty minutes in a woefully unsuccessful attempt to chop him down. The white flag of surrender was up in the air, waving violently. But the fun and games had only just begun. Luke was full of running.

As Alan Giles prepared to take the goal-kick, Luke sprinted back towards his own penalty area.

'Yeah,' he said.

Alan side-footed the ball to Luke's feet. He had time to turn and take a look. The red team backed off towards the halfway line. Luke took advantage of the space in front of him and dribbled forward unchallenged. He rode a half-hearted tackle from a red midfielder as he moved across the halfway line.

Swayne and Casey backed off towards their own penalty area.

'Tackle him,' Swayne said, screaming at his team-mates.

At last Luke faced some spirited resistance. The reds' midfield chased and tackled him, but Luke weaved his way forward, keeping the ball under sublime close control. His team-mates watched in amazement as Luke cut through the red team like a hot knife through butter.

Jerome had almost started to drool on the touchline as Luke approached the penalty area. Swayne dropped off, inviting Casey to move forward and attack the ball. Luke saw the laboured swipe of Niall Casey's right leg a mile off. He gently prodded the ball through Casey's legs, leaving him red-faced, sitting on the muddy floor.

Luke was now one-on-one with Swayne; time to rub it in. The shoddy defending of his team-mates left Peter Swayne open for the ultimate humiliation.

'Sweet baby Jesus,' Jerome said, whispering in a soft voice.

Luke stepped over the ball, rolling it onto his right heel and flicking it clean over Swayne's head. The last time Jerome had seen it done was in *Escape To Victory*, the football movie starring Michael Caine and Sylvester Stalone. He had never known anyone, even George Best, to perform such a dazzling piece of trickery in a real match. Swayne would have punched Luke in the head or grabbed hold of his jersey if he wasn't frozen to the spot in disbelief.

Everyone, apart from the red keeper, watched in silence as Luke took the ball on the volley and smashed it into the top right-hand corner. It went in off the crossbar.

Even Cecilia, who had never watched a football match before in her life, knew it was something special. Jerome pressed the palms of his hands together and whispered a quiet prayer.

'Please God. Tell me he's not signed.'

It was the best day ever. Even a successful four-year career with Rathdale Athletic had failed to thrust Luke into the spotlight the way that fourth goal had. As the match ended, Swayne and Co trotted off the pitch in disgust.

Luke was surrounded by his team-mates. Everyone was talking at once, laughing, smiling, patting his back, describing their view of the final goal.

Although Luke had played the match for selfish reasons, it had helped lift everyone's day.

'Make way, chaps,' Jerome said.

He cut his way through the crowd like a snowplough. Jerome stood before Luke with a smile as broad as O'Connell Street bridge. He stuck out a giant-sized hand.

'A privilege, Luke. An absolute privilege. I'm Jerome Barnes,' he said.

Luke refused the handshake. He glanced at Ella briefly. She tucked her hands into her duffel coat pockets and wore a dispassionate facial expression that matched her unimpressed stance. Luke turned his attention back to Jerome.

'I don't know whether the lads have mentioned it. But I manage a team,' Jerome said.

Again Luke made no effort to reply. Jerome's smile had subsided into an anxious grin. He had no heart to ask the next question. But he wanted to end the agony.

'Do you play for a team?' he said fearfully.

Luke's team-mates held their breath and stared at him in silence. They awaited his answer with the kind of tension normally reserved for the ten-second countdown to a new millennium.

'No,' Luke replied, finally.

Jerome's smile returned. He felt like punching the air, doing a lap of honour and screaming out, 'Yessss,' at the top of his lungs. He winked at a couple of the blue team before asking confidently, 'How about signing for the Stretford Enders?'

'No thanks,' Luke replied without delay.

Everyone went deathly still, shell-shocked by his curt answer. Luke had already begun walking across the pitch towards the main building, his schoolbag draped across his left shoulder. The surreal manner in which Luke had casually turned down the chance to join the Stretford Enders paralysed Jerome like a scorpion sting.

He stood motionless in the centre-circle surrounded by the blue team. It was a good ten seconds before he decided to fight back.

'Hey, wait a minute.'

Jerome sprinted across the muddy pitch to catch up with

Luke. He blocked his path to the main building but had to walk backwards to carry on a discussion.

'Do you want to think about it?' he said.

'No,' Luke replied casually.

'Why not?'

Luke stopped walking. He looked Jerome straight in the eye. 'I don't want to play football,' he said quietly.

Everyone watched Luke disappear into the main building, wondering the same question. 'Why?' Jerome felt as if someone was playing a cruel practical joke on him. As the other members of the blue team collected their schoolbags from behind the goal and went back for afternoon classes, Ella tugged Jerome by the arm.

'Come on, Pop, we'll be late,' she said.

Jerome was distraught. It took him a good thirty seconds to move a muscle. The only thing he did in the interim was breathe in and out. His breath drifted off on the breeze in a smoky vapour trail.

Ella massaged his huge right arm back into life. Jerome felt up to moving again. He and Ella walked out of the school driveway in complete silence.

Luke kept a low profile after the game. Swayne and Co were preparing for him to stride about the school corridors that afternoon, reminding them of their embarrassing humiliation on the hour, every hour. But Luke knew the value of keeping his mouth shut.

The whole point of playing the match had been to make his point on the football pitch. To boast verbally would diminish the display. Instead, Luke went back to his old routine, keeping himself to himself. The only difference being, he could freely acknowledge Cecilia when she said hello.

*

'I believe you scored a cracking goal yesterday?' Mr Ambrose said.

Luke looked up from his desk and smiled.

'I got lucky,' he replied.

Mr Ambrose grunted a laugh, picked up his brown leather briefcase from the floor and carried it to the door of metal-work room one. He looked back at Luke before leaving and said, 'A modest teenager. Wonders will never cease.'

Luke waited for Mr Ambrose to shut the door before unpacking the parts of the Spitfire. He pinned the construction schematic to the desk and lined the different manuals up alongside. Luke took the assembly instructions from his schoolbag and tucked them inside his jacket pocket. He walked over to the door of metalwork room one.

Across the hall Ella was busy. She lay beneath the chassis of the silver Ford Capri with a torch in one hand and a wrench in the other. Today FM was on the radio in the background. Ella didn't notice Luke enter the room until she spied his Nike Air runners on the ground in front of her.

'What do you want?' she said coldly.

Luke felt a little uncomfortable talking to someone lying beneath a car. He chewed on his right thumbnail for a moment.

'I need to talk to you,' he said.

'Then talk.'

Luke spat a lump of thumbnail out onto the floor. He let out an anxious sigh in preparation and removed the assembly instructions from his jacket pocket.

'Face to face,' Luke said.

After a few seconds, Ella rolled out from beneath the body of the Ford Capri. She got to her feet and walked over to the sink. Luke watched her squirt some industrial cleansing liquid into the palms of her hands, wash them under the hot tap, then dry them with a paper towel. Ella looked his way.

'What's this all about?' she said.

'I want to make a deal,' Luke replied.

Ella threw the paper towel in a plastic bin near the sink.

'Go on,' she said.

Luke took three measured paces across the oil-soaked floor, carefully watching his step. He held out the assembly instructions. Ella snatched them from his hand and walked straight past Luke to the teacher's desk to change her glasses. Luke watched her studying the instructions.

'I need some help,' he said.

Ella looked up. 'Why me?' she replied.

Luke took a quick look about to check if anyone could hear. He wasn't too keen on this deal becoming public knowledge. Metalwork room two was deserted, the only sound was the crackle of 'Don't Look Back in Anger' spewing out of the radio speaker. Finally, Luke laid it on the line.

'You help me assemble the Spit. I'll play for The Stretford Enders.'

Ella shook her head in confusion.

'What's in it for me?' she said.

It was a very good question. Luke had simply assumed Ella would jump at the chance to help out her father and his football team.

'Your da's the manager,' Luke replied doubtfully.

'So?'

Ella laughed. Luke frowned. He snatched the instructions clean out of her hands.

'Forget about it then,' he said.

Ella watched him storm off across the room. 'Moody git,' she thought to herself. She waited for Luke to pull the door open before calling after him.

'I have to finish this job today,' Ella said.

Luke stopped. He held the door open and looked back in at Ella.

'18 Sycamore Street. Bring it over tomorrow, after school,' she said.

Ella had already disappeared back beneath the chassis of the Ford Capri before Luke could reply. He stood at the ajar door for a while longer.

'You've got training on Thursdays, half six, Woodlawn Park,' Ella said.

'Right,' Luke replied to the empty room.

'And a match Saturday morning.'

Luke nodded his head this time. He closed the door after him and went back across the corridor to metalwork room one with a large grin plastered across his face. It seemed like things were changing for the better.

Not only had he beaten off Swayne and Co. He had also managed to impress Cecilia, found someone to assemble the Spitfire and joined a football team in one fell swoop. Surely no one had managed to kill four birds with one stone. Luke gathered together his stuff and left metalwork room one.

Part of the Bargain

Luke had never heard of Sycamore Street before and had a great deal of trouble finding it. He wandered aimlessly around Woodlawn housing estate for twenty minutes, asking different people for directions.

Luke was moving closer to Bloomfield shopping centre when he stopped an old man on a push-bike.

'No, son. You're miles out,' the old man said.

He gave Luke a simple direction. 'Head for the fire station. You can spit onto Sycamore Street from there.'

It was top-notch advice. Luke knew exactly how to get to the fire station. It was right round the corner from Woodlawn Comprehensive. Ten short minutes later he reached Sycamore Street.

Luke counted the door numbers as he strolled down the wide concrete pavement, the rectangular Spitfire box tucked beneath his left armpit.

'Eighteen,' Luke said quietly.

Ella's house was on the corner of Sycamore Street, with a massive front garden. Luke walked past three separate cars blocking up the driveway. He pressed his finger against the doorbell outside the porch. While he waited for an answer, Luke glanced around the garden.

The lawn was neatly trimmed. Rose bushes, shrubs and delicate flower beds formed a leafy L inside the perimeter of the waist-high garden wall.

Luke's attention turned to the cars.

A brand-new bottle-green Ford Probe. Behind that an ancient canary-yellow Nissan Micra, and last of all was a glittery purple Volkswagen on concrete blocks.

'Wipe your feet,' Ella said.

Luke turned round. Ella was standing in the porch. He followed her inside, wiping his feet on a faded Man Utd rug. As they moved through the hallway to the kitchen, the muffled sound of music pounded the walls. Luke clicked his fingers.

'Tears of a Clown,' he said.

'It's my brother's band,' Ella replied.

She opened a sliding door at the back of a large kitchen extension. Luke stepped out into the garden. A nine foot high garden wall was camouflaged on each side by lanky pine trees. The abounding collection of potted plants and multi-coloured flower beds surrounding the lawn suggested a keen gardener in the family.

Luke followed Ella down a narrow path in the centre of the lawn to a large concrete shed at the back of the garden. She unlocked a massive black steel door.

As Ella swung the door open, 'Tears of a Clown' blasted across the neighbourhood. Ella and Luke went inside. But 'Tears of a Clown' had quickly dripped to a halt. The members of the Funky Starfish stared at them with obvious contempt. The bass player led the calls of disgust.

'Hurry up,' he said, shouting angrily.

Ella ignored his moody cry. She casually led Luke across the spacious rehearsal room. The walls and ceiling were covered in long strips of carpet, empty blue egg cartons and thick white slabs of foam.

Luke took a quick glance at the bass player. He was tall, black, thin and extremely good-looking. He wore a white silk shirt with a picture of a red and green Chinese dragon across the chest, snow white Levi flares and black leather boots. The four other band members had similar taste in fashion. Flared corduroy trousers, vintage leather jackets, silk shirts, old-style Adidas canvas trainers. They all sported thick sideburns, scruffy mop-top haircuts or, in the bass player's case, a groovy afro.

Luke waited until he and Ella passed through a door on the other side of the room before asking a few questions.

'Who are they?'

'The Funky Starfish. The bass player is my brother, Isaac,' Ella replied.

Luke nodded his head. It was only now he noticed the décor of the new room. It was long and narrow, not much bigger than a cubicle in a school toilet. As Ella took the rectangular box from under Luke's arm, he took a good look around. There was a sturdy brown desk in front of them, with a small red table lamp.

'Take a seat,' Ella said.

Luke pulled up a wooden stool. The rest of the room, which wasn't much, was made up of metal tool boxes and car manuals stacked high in the corners. Manchester City posters covered every inch of the bare concrete walls.

The centre-piece of her shrine to City was a framed photograph, on the desk, of the victorious Division Two play-off winners celebrating their penalty shoot-out win over Gillingham in May 1999. A Sony portable stereo sat at the foot of the desk, a small pile of CDs by its side. As the Funky Starfish broke back into life with another faultless rendition of the Smoky Robinson classic, 'Tears of a Clown', Luke bent down to examine Ella's taste in music.

'Do you have the parts list?' she said.

Luke looked up. Ella had the construction schematic,

assembly instructions and radio-control manual laid out on the desk.

'Is it not there?' Luke replied over the loud din.

Ella shook her head.

Out in the rehearsal room, The Funky Starfish were halfway through 'Tears of a Clown'. Isaac sang lead vocals in a sweet falsetto voice. Gubby the keyboard player and Dan the drummer sang backing harmonies.

'If I appear to be carefree, It's only to cover-up my sadness. In order to shield my pride I try . . .'

Ella opened the repair room door. She and Luke waited to cut across the rehearsal room a second time. This caused Isaac to lose concentration. He nearly threw his bass guitar on the floor in anger.

'Woah, woah, woah.'

Isaac suspended the Starfish with a frenzied wave of his left hand.

'Ella,' he said loudly.

'What?' she replied.

Isaac escorted his little sister across the rehearsal room by the arm. He flung the steel door open wide for her and Luke to leave.

'No more interruptions,' he said.

Ella stepped back into the garden, but Luke stayed put. He stood face to face with Isaac. It was obvious Luke had something to say, but Isaac had no intention of entering into a polite conversation. The other members of the Funky Starfish stared at the stand-off. Isaac finally lost his patience.

'What?' he said rudely.

Luke sang in a croaky falsetto voice, 'If I appear to be carefree, it's only to CAM-O-FLAGUE my sadness.'

Isaac and his fellow Funky Starfish looked at one another. Luke had stunned them into an embarrassing silence.

Before he could reply, Luke closed the steel door in Isaac's face. Ella waited for him by the porch.

'What was all that about?' she said.

'Just putting him straight about Smoky,' Luke replied.

The journey from Sycamore Street to Montague Avenue passed off in silence. The occasional remark was made about assembling the model Spitfire. But Luke decided to keep the reason behind his mission a secret. After all, a brief description of his master plan had inspired a potent mixture of confusion and boredom in Cecilia.

All Ella needed to know was Luke wanted the Spitfire assembled. In return he would play for The Stretford Enders, end of story. Luke felt a sharp shiver shoot up his spine at the thought of it. What a stupid name for a football team.

'Why are they called The Stretford Enders?' he said.

Ella looked his way briefly.

'My dad's from Manchester. He says he grew up standing on the Stretford End.'

Luke studied Ella carefully. He sensed her explanation was far from finished.

'He played for United as well. In the reserves.'

Luke hated Man Utd with a deep-rooted passion. But anyone good enough to play for such a big football team deserved some respect. As they walked down Montague Avenue, Luke thought of another question.

'Why do you support City?'

Ella didn't answer straightaway. It was only when Luke opened the front door to Mrs Hendy's house that he got a reply.

'To annoy me dad,' she said.

Luke invited Ella inside. He spent the journey from the front door to the first floor trying to work out the meaning behind her answer. Ella was dreading the thought of Luke's barrage of follow-on personal questions. She decided to jump in with a counter-attack.

'Why do you support Everton?'

Luke went silent. He didn't seem able to answer. This was better; Ella puffed an invisible sigh of relief as Luke opened the door. They went inside. Now it was Ella's turn to be nosy. She picked up a picture frame from the top of the TV set. It was a photograph of Martina and Luke standing on a beach. '*Portmarnock, June 98*' was written in the bottom right hand corner of the frame. Luke was wearing white shorts with no T-shirt. He was extremely thin, but had a muscular physique.

'Catch,' Luke said.

Ella looked up. Luke tossed something across to her. It was the parts list. For a moment their eyes locked. Ella had fabulous chocolate-brown eyes, so dark and elusive. Luke knew he should, but he couldn't look away. Ella felt the same, but she had more self-discipline. She quickly moved her gaze to the job at hand.

'What's this model aeroplane for?' she said.

This was a question Luke wanted to avoid answering.

'Do you really need to know?' he replied defensively.

Ella looked down at the parts list. 'I was just asking,' she said quietly, flicking through the pages.

The sharp click of the front door lock made her look up. Luke was holding the door open, waiting for Ella to leave. Surely he hadn't taken offence from such a straightforward question.

'What?' Ella asked.

Luke wore a slight smile.

'We're going for tea and cake.'

*

Luke and Ella sat on the couch in the back parlour, a polite distance apart. Mrs Hendy had just popped out to the toilet. Luke took the opportunity to explain things.

'See, Jimmy was a fighter pilot. But he died in the Battle of Britain.'

Luke plucked the photograph of Jimmy from the top of the piano. He handed it to Ella. After a while, he held his hand out to take it back and returned it to the piano.

When Luke sat back down beside Ella on the couch, he had moved a few inches closer to her. Luke didn't seem to notice this change, but Ella couldn't help but watch their knees. They were inches from touching.

'So, what I want to do is . . .'

Mrs Hendy came back into the parlour before Luke could finish his explanation. She sat down on her armchair with a notepad and pencil in her hands. She was busy making a shopping list. She muttered to herself about eggs, sugar and tin foil as she scribbled away.

While she wrote out her shopping list, Luke caught sight of his knees, they were in danger of knocking against Ella's.

Luke couldn't help looking up, it was a reflex action. When he did, he found Ella staring straight back at him. He could feel her breath on his face. It made him gulp nervously. The awkward silence was broken by Mrs Hendy's timely cough. Luke and Ella jumped to their feet simultaneously.

'Now, remember to get yourselves something nice,' she said, smiling.

Luke and Ella quickly made their way from the back parlour and headed straight out onto Montague Avenue. As they walked to Iceland on Main Street, Ella started to get her head around Luke's plan.

'So, I assemble the Spitfire,' she said.

Luke nodded his head.

'Then you bring Mrs Hendy out to Howth to see it fly.'

Luke didn't reply. He had already explained this to her. He got the feeling she was about to laugh at him or rubbish his plan. Ella followed Luke through the main entrance to Iceland. He picked up a green shopping basket and studied Mrs Hendy's shopping list. Ella asked another question.

'Why?' she said.

Luke looked up from the list.

'Why what?'

'Why are you doing this?'

It was a tough one. Luke had no intention of opening up his true feelings, not to a virtual stranger. Ella trailed him around the aisles, awaiting a reply. It was obvious Luke was trying to avoid the question by concentrating on Mrs Hendy's shopping list. But Ella was determined to squeeze it out of him. Eventually he gave up and shared the truth.

'Look, Mrs H is the only friend I have in Dun Laoghaire,' Luke said.

As he walked off down the biscuit aisle and examined the different prices for custard creams and jammy dodgers, Ella asked another question.

'What about Cecilia?' she said.

Luke took a packet of rich tea biscuits from the top shelf and paid close attention to the ingredients list. Ella started to feel uncomfortable; she regretted asking the question. They spent an agonising six seconds in silence before Ella said, 'Do you need bread?'

'Two slice pans,' Luke replied instantly.

Ella walked off down the biscuit aisle. Luke looked up from the packet of rich tea to see her go. She tucked her hands deep into the pockets of her duffel coat and turned off the biscuit aisle.

As she turned, Luke caught a glimpse of her neck. It was beautiful. So slender and elegant. The clothes Ella wore were an obvious attempt to cover up every inch of her body. Luke didn't know why, she wasn't ugly.

He plonked a packet of custard creams into the shopping basket before making his way into the frozen food section.

Mrs Hendy gave Ella and Luke a pound each as a reward for their trip to Iceland. After helping her pack away the messages, Luke invited Ella back to his bedroom for a mug of tea and a chat about the Spitfire.

'Sugar?' Luke asked.

'No thanks.'

She was sitting on Luke's bed, flicking through a cardboard box full of old records. Luke came into the bedroom, holding the two mugs of tea. He placed Ella's on the bedside cabinet and sipped his own.

'Are all these yours?' Ella said.

'No, well, yeah. They're me da's,' Luke replied.

Ella took a sip of her tea as Luke sat down on the bed beside her. He pulled out a copy of Marvin Gaye's album *What's Going On*. Luke touched the plastic sleeve with the tips of his fingers before looking at Ella.

'Will I put it on?' he said.

Ella shrugged her shoulders. Luke seemed a little disappointed with her reply.

'Yeah, put it on,' Ella said brightly, realising her initial reaction was rude.

Luke smiled. He walked across to an old record player sitting on a wooden chair by the radiator. He slid the vinyl from the record sleeve with gentle care, making sure to grip it by the edges.

'In case you're wondering, I have heard of CDs. But me da

always said nothing plays better than vinyl,' Luke said with a smile.

He flicked the RPM switch to 33 and carefully brought the needle down on the run-in groove. The first sound to come out of the speaker was a soft crackling hiss. This quickly gave way to the sweet soul music of Marvin Gaye. Luke nodded his head in time with the funky saxophone. Ella sipped her tea.

'Where's your dad now?' she said.

Luke stopped moving his head. He took hold of the record sleeve for comfort, like a child holding a security blanket.

'He left,' Luke said quietly.

Ella felt guilty for asking such a personal question. She wanted to apologise, but then decided that might make matters worse. Instead, Ella started flicking through the records. She stopped at a sleeve with the title 'We All Love Everton: FA Cup Final 1985'.

'Your dad supported Everton?' Ella said.

Luke turned round to look at her. He was wearing an unusual smile. Ella started to feel self-conscious.

'What?' she said.

Luke lowered the volume on the record player. He walked forward and lifted the cardboard box out of Ella's lap. He started flicking through the records, searching for one in particular.

'Why did your folks call you Ella?' Luke said.

He continued flicking through the records. Ella watched in silence, finally she answered.

'They named me after some old jazz singer.'

Luke nodded his head, continuing with his search. Suddenly, he stopped. He plucked a record sleeve from the centre of the stack and handed it to Ella. She looked at the picture on the cover. It was of a pretty black woman holding a microphone. She wore a red beret and glasses with orange coloured lenses. '*Ella Fitzgerald Sings*'.

Ella wasn't impressed. She quickly handed the sleeve back to Luke then reached over for her mug and gulped the last of her tea. Luke stared at her a while before asking.

'Will I put it on?'

Ella shook her head to signal an emphatic no. It was an embarrassing situation. But it seemed pointless to argue. Anyway, Luke was already removing the Marvin Gaye record and replacing it with Ella Fitzgerald. As he placed the needle on the run-in groove, the anticipation was becoming unbearable. Ella picked up the record sleeve again and read the title of the first song. 'Someone to Watch Over Me'. Luke turned towards her as the crackling hiss gave way to music. It was a beautiful ballad with an orchestra accompanying the singer. Luke and Ella listened in total silence.

Martina gasped with exhaustion as she carried four plastic bags up the staircase. It was her first night off in weeks and her only reward was a trip to Tesco's for groceries. As she dumped the bags on the floor outside the room and fiddled around inside her jacket pocket for her key, the sound of music drifted through the walls.

'Ella Fitzgerald,' she said to herself quietly.

Martina opened the front door and carried the bags inside. 'Luke,' she said.

His bedroom door was shut tight and the living room was drenched in darkness. Martina switched on the lights and looked about the room. There was something unsettling about its undisturbed nature. No smell of glue, no pieces of wood and rolls of blue paper sprawled across the floor.

Martina walked across to the bedroom door. Despite the deep embarrassment and horror she, and Luke, could face by walking in unannounced, it was a risk she was willing to take. Martina took a deep breath, pressed down on the door handle and swung it open.

'Ma,' Luke said.

Martina was confronted by the sight of Ella and Luke, innocently sitting side by side on his bed. They looked at each other briefly. Martina walked across to the record player and lowered the volume. Luke got up from the bed, he looked between Ella and Martina. The longer they remained silent, the more awkward things would become.

'Ma, this is me friend, Ella. Ella, this is me Ma,' Luke said.

Ella fought a smile off her face. Luke considered her a friend. She sat up from the bed, left her mug of tea on the cabinet and reached out her right hand.

'Hello,' Ella said shyly.

Martina shook her hand, but didn't reply verbally.

'We'd better go,' Luke said.

Martina left the bedroom first. Ella picked up the *Ella Fitzgerald Sings* record sleeve from Luke's bed.

'Can I borrow this?' she said.

Luke was surprised how quickly she had taken to the sound of her namesake. But he nodded his head positively. He walked across to the record player and gently lifted the needle. He stopped the motor and removed the vinyl with the same gentle care as before, sliding it back into the sleeve.

'Be careful with it,' Luke said.

Ella nodded her head as a reply, concentrating her interest on the record sleeve. She followed Luke into the living room and gathered together her duffel coat and the parts list. Martina watched them all the way, but never said a single word.

'Bye,' Ella said quietly as she left.

Martina didn't reply. She just smiled awkwardly and

semi-nodded her head. Luke looked back at his mother in confusion. It wasn't like her to be nervous around new people, especially in her own home.

Although she insisted on walking home alone, Luke stayed with Ella until they reached the roundabout that separated Harbour Road and Sycamore Street. The wind blew hard, rain drizzled down and a row of orange street-lamps blinked on and shone brightly, signalling the start of the night.

'We'll talk about the Spitfire tomorrow, after the match,' Luke said.

He turned to leave, but quickly looked back at Ella.

'Are you coming to the match?' he said.

Ella took her keys out from an inside pocket in her duffel coat. She walked into her front garden and opened the porch door before shouting back.

'Maybe.'

Luke shook his head as Ella disappeared behind her front door. 'Why do girls do that?' he said to himself as he started back down Harbour Road.

Repaying the Debt

Technically, it was all part of a deal to assemble the Spitfire. But as Luke left Mrs Hendy's boarding house the next morning at nine o'clock, he felt like a million dollars. There was nothing to match the excitement of playing a football match.

Even Montague Avenue seemed a bright and cheerful place as Luke closed the front door, skipped down the concrete steps and swung his schoolbag over his shoulder.

It had taken him forty minutes to dump his schoolbooks onto his bed, scrub and polish his Nike football boots, find his Umbro-Pro shinguards and nag Martina out of bed to help find his Everton football socks.

'Clean those boots before you come back inside,' Martina said.

She crawled back into her bedroom. It was her first Saturday off work in weeks. Luke did a quick vocal impression of her prat boyfriend Ronald.

'Yes, of course,' he said quietly.

Luke had no trouble imitating a Dutch accent thanks to the large presence of Dutch players and managers in English football. Hasselbaink, Bergkamp, Stam, it was a simple case of listen and repeat. The 'yes, of course' bit was a mockery of Ronald's favourite phrase, which he was guaranteed to spout once every half-hour.

Despite a quick shudder at the thought of Ronald's garish

tie collection, Luke was determined to approach the game in a positive frame of mind.

He stopped off at Kelly's newsagents on Woodlawn Drive to buy his trusty half-time snack. Two bananas and a bottle of Lucozade Sport were the perfect pick-me-up to keep you running through the second-half of a game. As Luke reached the school gates, he spotted Jerome and Ella at the goal-posts, putting up the nets.

'Alright, Luke,' a voice said.

Luke swung round. It was Copper Martin, the red-headed kid who'd played for the blue bibs in the lunch-time match against Swayne and Co.

'Alright,' he replied awkwardly.

Luke had forgotten Copper's first name. He didn't know what to call him.

'Are you coming in?' Copper said.

Luke stood at the gates for a moment; the beep of a car horn made up his mind for him. A large silver Mercedes was waiting to pass by. Luke and Copper stood aside as it drove into the car park.

Copper walked over to where the Mercedes was parking. Luke waited for a while before deciding to follow. The sight of Cecilia climbing out of the back seat made his mind up for him. He felt his heartbeat accelerate out of control. Alan Giles jumped out of the front passenger seat. He had his goalkeeper gloves on already.

'HONCHEE!!!' Swayne said loudly.

Luke stepped onto the path to avoid a collision. Swayne and Co zoomed past on their mountain bikes.

'Oh no,' Luke said quietly.

His first training session with the Stretford Enders had been scheduled for Thursday evening but had been cancelled due to a torrential rain storm. For Luke, this was a welcome delay from the harsh reality.

Swayne and Co were his new team-mates. That was a problem for two reasons. First of all, they'd probably spend more time kicking him than the opposing forwards. And secondly, if they defended like they did on Thursday, Luke would probably spend most of his time defending in his own penalty area.

A stream of cars pulled into the car park one after another. Luke watched Copper, Alan and Cecilia walking past the bike shed. Swayne said something to her as she passed by, she didn't reply.

Luke and Swayne locked stares. 'He'll probably blame that on me as well,' Luke thought to himself as he cut through the basketball courts to reach the football pitch.

Luke stood in the centre-circle with Jerome and his team-mates; Copper, David, Alan Giles and Swayne and Co. This was the team. They had three substitutes – two chubby kids with pudding bowl haircuts who looked like twin brothers and a tiny blond kid with glasses, an inhaler and a copy of *Sci-Fi World* magazine.

'OK, boys. We'll go with the hammerhead today,' Jerome said.

'The what?' Luke replied, interrupting the manager's flow.

Jerome wasn't upset. He smiled, walked across to Luke and slung his arm round his shoulder.

'It's my own formation. 3–1–1–2–1–2,' he said proudly.

He produced a piece of yellow notepaper from a pocket on his Man Utd promo jacket. It was a team-sheet, lined out in his infamous hammerhead formation.

Luke stared at the team-sheet, then back at Jerome in mild disbelief. It made no sense whatsoever. There was a three-man defence, four in midfield and three centre-forwards. They would get creamed playing this formation.

Jerome patted Luke's shoulder, leaving him with the notepaper. He pointed to two members of Co.

'You play up front, just behind Alex and Lorcan.'

Luke wanted to ask questions but Jerome sauntered away to the touchline before he got the chance to speak. He looked back at the team-sheet. 'Where am I playing?' he thought to himself. It was hard to tell if he was a centre-forward or an attacking midfielder.

Swayne was busy telling one of his dirty jokes to Co when Jerome walked back into the centre-circle. He unwrapped two sticks of spearmint chewing gum and chucked them into his mouth. He handed the empty wrappers to Ella. Everyone fell silent as he clapped his hands together twice. He looked at his players in silence. The only sound a squelching noise as he chewed the gum. He pointed his right index finger across at the boys from St David's FC.

'They're afraid of you,' Jerome said.

Luke watched in bemusement as the manager sauntered back towards the touchline, hands behind his back. Swayne barged Luke out of the way as he entered the scramble for jerseys. It was like a pig sty, everyone fighting for a piece of the action.

Luke turned his attention back to the team-sheet.

'It looks nothing like a hammerhead shark,' he said quietly.

'Luke,' Alan Giles said.

He threw a jersey over to him. Luke held the jersey up to the dim sunlight. He was truly disgusted.

'What's this?' he said abruptly.

Luke never got an answer. His team-mates were already decked out in a Manchester United away kit from season 90–91. It was a horrible royal-blue jersey with streaky white flashes. Alan Giles had given him the No.8 jersey, even though he was listed as No.9 on the team-sheet. He stood still, staring at the jersey for a full minute before eventually pulling it over his head.

'OK,' Luke said calmly.

He took deep breaths and tried to stay positive. After all, Rathdale Athletic's under-fourteens were one of the top schoolboy sides in Dublin. Mr O'Driscoll treated his players like professionals. The Stretford Enders were . . . different.

As the team lined out, Luke noticed Swayne and Casey playing as centre-half and sweeper. David Swayne was stuck at right-back and Copper Martin seemed to be standing somewhere between defence and midfield. St David's lined out as a typical 4–4–2. Over on the touchline, Cecilia and Ella stood ten yards apart. Ella had her headphones on and kept her hands in her pockets. Occasionally she looked Luke's way.

Cecilia kept a similar low profile. But any time their eyes met, she wore a subtle grin. Jerome pointed at the three substitutes. They each took a football and dribbled down the touchline. The referee placed the whistle in his mouth. As he blew, Luke mumbled to himself.

'We're gonna get slaughtered.'

'Settle on it, settle on it,' Jerome said, his hands cupped around his mouth.

As he stood screaming this pearl of wisdom, Niall Casey lost his concentration. The St David's No.9 pinched the ball off Casey's left boot and steamed towards Alan Giles in goal. It took a beautifully timed challenge from David Swayne to prevent a certain goal.

'OK, Enders, second ball. Clear the second ball,' Jerome said.

Luke stood on the penalty spot marking the St David's

No.5. 'Second ball? We can't even clear the first one,' he thought to himself. As the corner came swinging into the near post, Alan Giles cried out.

'Keeper's ball.'

He proceeded to punch fresh air, leaving the St David's No.10 with a simple header into the back of the net. Stretford Enders O: St David's 4.

Jerome lost it. He tore off his lucky black bobble hat, flung it on the ground and trampled it into the mud. Ella shook her head with embarrassment while Cecilia looked predictably confused by the action on the pitch. Four of her school friends had joined her on the touchline.

'Come on, Luke,' she said supportively.

Luke walked up to Alex and Lorcan in the centre-circle.

'Knock it back to Swayne,' he said.

They didn't pay him any attention. But Luke was determined to try. He jogged back towards Swayne and Casey.

'Knock it over the top. I'll run onto it,' he said.

'Piss off, Honchee,' Swayne replied without delay.

Luke shook his head in frustration. Copper Martin and David Swayne were the only players on the pitch who seemed interested in passing to him.

'Come on, Enders, lift it,' Jerome said.

The referee blew his whistle and Lorcan tipped off. Alex knocked the ball back towards Casey. Luke made sure it didn't reach him.

'Hey,' Casey said in disgust.

Swayne and Co watched as Luke intercepted the back pass and steamed up the left wing. St David's were a well-disciplined team and their midfielders tracked him carefully. He reached the halfway line, but there was no way through the mass of defenders in front of him.

'Luke,' a voice said.

Copper was in space, ten yards behind him. Luke laid the ball off to him and sprinted down the left wing. It was an all or nothing move. Copper had no time to think about it as the St David's No.9 chased across to tackle him. He launched the ball forward, over the heads of the St David's defence.

As the ball dropped down outside the penalty area, Luke was in a straight race for possession with the No.2 and the No.4. It all depended on who got the first touch. As the No.4 prepared to hack the ball clear, Luke stuck out his right toe and managed to turn it past him. It wrong-footed the No.4 completely and left Luke with a clear run on goal.

He sprinted into the penalty area with the No.2 in close attendance. The angle for a shot wasn't great, as the goal-keeper had come out to narrow it.

However, the other centre-half, No.5, had come across to cover the No.4's mistake. This left Alex unmarked behind him. Luke side-footed the ball across the penalty area, taking the goalkeeper and No.5 out of the game.

Alex had an open goal and easily slotted the ball home from fourteen yards. Stretford Enders 1: St David's 4. Alex took to a lap of honour, receiving the congratulations of Swayne and Co. Only Copper made a run for Luke.

'Great play,' he said.

Luke smiled, shook his hand, then jogged back to the halfway line.

'Skill, vision, generosity . . . What a player,' Jerome said, smiling.

Ella felt her father was exaggerating. She let out an unimpressed tut. Cecilia and her gang had gradually edged closer to Jerome. They were standing right beside him now. Every time he made a positive remark about Luke, Cecilia produced those pearly whites with a sugar-sweet smile. But as the game wore on, Ella noticed that Cecilia spent most of her time talking to her friends about her forthcoming appearance on *Star Search 2000*. She only turned to the pitch when she heard Jerome shout with excitement.

'Peter,' he said, groaning in despair.

It couldn't have been more than forty seconds since Alex scored down the other end. But already, inept defending had cost the Enders another goal.

This time Peter Swayne deluded himself into thinking he could dribble out of defence like Marcel Desailly or Franco Baresi. What actually happened was a clumsy fifteen yard run before he lost control of the ball, stumbled and fell over. This left the St David's No.9 with a simple chance to claim a first-half hat-trick. Enders 1: St David's 5.

'What are you doing?' Jerome said loudly.

Swayne got to his feet and placed his hands on his hips. Luke sighed desperately. Surely it couldn't get much worse? Seconds after he said this to himself, Casey mis-kicked a simple clearance straight to their No.9. Alan Giles managed to pull off a brilliant reflex save, but he couldn't do anything about the rebound. Enders 1: St David's 6.

'Aarrgghh-geehhh-urrghhh-arhhdghhh.'

Jerome was so angry now he couldn't even shout real words. His fury and frustration melted into one continuous sound. He growled like a lion trying to eat a gazelle with a knife and fork. The referee blew the whistle to signal half-time. As the Enders walked to the touchline, the sight of Jerome pacing up and down impatiently was a little unnerving.

'What in the name of sweet-baby-Jesus was that?' he said, in a slow and eerily gentle tone.

No one had an answer. Swayne slugged from the Ballygowen water bottle while Casey picked lumps of mud from the studs on his boots.

Luke walked over to the kit bag. He took out his half-time snack and munched into the first banana. Cecilia was standing ten feet behind Jerome. She smiled at him. But Luke was more interested in Ella. He tipped her on the left shoulder. She removed her headphones.

'Are they always this bad?' he said quietly.

Ella pondered her reply carefully. Finally, she said, 'They *did* win a game in October.'

Luke watched her stroll away. She passed by Jerome, the other players, and finally Cecilia and friends.

Cecilia wore a cheeky grin. She lifted her right hand slightly towards him. It was like a domino effect. Luke knew Swayne had seen this, and he knew Swayne would be drilling a hole through the back of his skull with an evil stare.

Luke unscrewed the cap from his bottle of Lucozade Sport. He gulped it down while watching Jerome's animated half-time talk. He threw his arms about violently, rubbed his fingers through his hair, pointed at players, shouted at players, kept repeating phrases like, 'Look up', 'Keep it tight', 'Create the space'.

'Luke, where's Luke?' Jerome said frantically.

Luke walked forward to rejoin the semi-circle of players. Jerome pointed at him.

'Alex, Lorcan, back into midfield. Luke, up on your own.'

This news was greeted with expressions of jealousy and muttered disgust. Swayne and Co had no intention of playing the ball up front to Luke so he could grab the glory. Jerome snatched the water bottle away from Casey and took a frenzied swig. Holding his left hand in the air, he gave his instructions for the second-half.

'Here's the plan. Knock-the-ball-to-Luke. Understand?'

The Enders mumbled yes. They trotted back onto the

pitch for the second-half. Swayne moved close to Luke for a quiet word in his ear.

'You're dead, Honchee,' he said.

For a while, there was hope. Three minutes into the second-half, Luke controlled a long clearance from Casey on his chest ten yards outside their penalty area. Somehow, he managed to weave his way past four well-timed tackles. He was now inside the penalty area, one-on-one with the goalkeeper.

His run on goal was no formality. The keeper sprinted from his line and spread himself well. But Luke had the composure to chip the ball over his outstretched right glove into the back of the net. Enders 2: St David's 6. Jerome clapped, Cecilia and her gang cheered, but Swayne and Co remained icy.

As the second-half wore on, the Enders came into the game more and more. It seemed like the St David's players were tired from their continuous attacking in the first-half. Luke was getting a lot more of the ball, but the St David's defence stuck to their task well and gave him only one more clear chance to score. It was a corner, swung across from David Swayne. The No.5 headed it clear.

'Whack it, son, whack it,' Jerome said, whispering to himself.

The No.5's looping header fell to Luke on the edge of the penalty area. It seemed like he read Jerome's mind, volleying the ball sweetly with his right boot. As soon as he hit it, it was going into the top left-hand corner. Enders 3: St David's 6.

'Yessss,' Jerome said, dancing about the touchline in sheer delight.

As St David's kicked off, it seemed like the Enders could score again. But the match suddenly fell into a dull stalemate. St David's began to pass the ball about neatly. They worked hard to win back possession in midfield and gradually pushed the Enders back towards their own penalty area. It was only a matter of time before they grabbed a seventh goal. It came with four minutes left on the clock; another unforced error from Peter Swayne. Enders 3: St David's 7.

As the referee blew the final whistle, Jerome took a seat on the kit bag. Luke shook hands with the players from St David's, receiving the odd comment of 'good goal' and 'well done'. By the time he made his way off the pitch, Jerome and Swayne were screaming into each other's faces.

'You're not fit to captain this side,' Jerome said angrily.

Swayne was outraged. He tore off his captain's armband and jersey and flung them at Jerome's chest.

'Stuff you and your poxy team,' he said.

The other Enders watched as Swayne walked across the basketball court, naked from the waist up. Casey and Co decided to make a stand with their captain. Each one took off his jersey and threw it at Jerome's feet, without uttering a single word.

Eventually, only seven players remained. Alan Giles, David Swayne, Copper Martin and Luke. Then the substitutes, Gerard Burke, Philip Burke and Edgar O'Lone.

'Nice one,' Luke said to himself.

It seemed the curse was set to continue. So far, everything he had come into contact with in Dun Laoghaire exploded in his face like a bomb. Still, quite a record. One game, two goals, team disbanded.

'Copper, open the dressing rooms,' Jerome said, tossing him the keys.

Luke followed his remaining team-mates into the dressing rooms in silence. As they walked forward slowly, heads bowed, hearts low, boots clucking against the concrete pavement, Luke had an idea.

In the aftermath of the defeat, and what Luke didn't witness as he shook hands with the players from St David's, was Peter Swayne performing one of his trademark moans. Blaming the defeat on his team-mates, bad management, the length of the grass. Arrogant bellyaching from Swayne was commonplace after an Enders' defeat. But this time, Jerome snapped.

It led to a decision. Jerome told Swayne he was no longer captain, that job belonged to Luke. Swayne replied to this bombshell by quitting the Enders, taking Casey and five other players along with him. As things stood, the worst team in the South Dublin District league were in a spot of bother.

'That's it then. No more team,' Alan said sadly.

Copper fastened the belt buckle on his white Levi jeans.

'What difference does it make? We haven't won a game for five months,' he said.

Gerard Burke, or Muffin to his friends, sat beside Luke, eating a king-size packet of Skips while reading the football section of the *Daily Star*.

'We might have done with Luke in the side,' he said.

Muffin looked up at Luke, smiling. He shuffled his packet of Skips. Luke took a handful, but before eating them, he asked.

'Are there any other football teams in Dun Laoghaire?'

Everyone shook their heads.

'The nearest team is Dalkey United,' Alan replied.

Luke took a quick head count. They had seven players, four short of a team. As he munched down the Skips, Jerome walked into the dressing room, bobble hat in hand. Everyone fell silent. Ella stood outside. She looked in at Luke before Jerome shut the door.

'Lads. I'm here to offer my resignation,' he said quietly.

Jerome pinned a sheet of white paper to the back of the dressingroom door. He took one last look at his remaining players. When he reached Luke, he smiled and stuck out his right hand.

'Thanks for coming along, Luke,' Jerome said.

They shook hands. The boys watched in silence as Jerome put on his bobble hat, gathered together the kit bag, water bottles and footballs and left the dressing room without a whisper.

Everyone sat in silence, unable to talk or move, stunned into a trance. Such a sad display was enough to convince Luke he could do it. He stood up, walked over to the door, ripped the resignation note into tiny pieces and threw it in the bin.

'This isn't over yet,' he said. 'Meet me here, Monday morning. Ten to nine.'

He looked about the remaining Stretford Enders, all of whom nodded their heads in agreement. Luke left the dressing room without uttering another word. No one asked him why they were meeting on Monday morning, probably because no one doubted Luke Farrell. Somehow, it seemed as though he was sent to save the Stretford Enders.

Outside the dressing rooms, Ella stood waiting to discuss the Spitfire. Luke was more interested in Jerome.

'Where's your da gone?' he said.

'Work,' Ella replied.

Luke walked forward aimlessly, heading in the general direction of the basketball courts. Ella followed on. She pulled a Spitfire assembly schedule from her duffel coat pocket, one she had drawn up the night before. Luke caught sight of the schedule.

'Not now, Ella. We'll talk later,' he said.

He walked off towards the car park. As he crossed the first basketball court he noticed Jerome driving his bottle-green Ford Probe out of the school gates onto Woodlawn Drive.

Luke stood alone on the basketball court, scuffing his trainers against the wet tarmac, wondering what to do next.

'Luke.'

Cecilia was standing in the car park alone. Her friends were walking out of the driveway. This time she didn't bother to wave. Luke stood and watched in amazement as she ran, actually *ran*, across the damp grass to meet him.

'Hi,' she said, gasping for breath.

Luke was dumbstruck. Cecilia was wearing a silver bubble jacket, black hipsters, black leather boots, a red scarf and a grey bobble hat. She smiled and let out a little laugh as she brushed some strands of hair away from her face.

'Thanks for coming,' Luke said nervously.

Cecilia didn't reply. She slowly moved forward, grasping his tracksuit top with both her hands. He could feel her warm breath on his face. She moved her head slightly to the right, edged forward and kissed him. Luke had never been kissed before, but he quickly got the hang of it. He closed his eyes and gently pressed his lips against hers.

Three sharp beeps of a car horn ended their embrace. Luke noticed the silver Mercedes waiting in the car park. Cecilia pressed her palm against his chest.

'See you around,' she said softly.

Luke didn't reply, but he nodded his head six or seven times. Cecilia walked across the damp grass, heading towards the car park. It took two or three minutes for the reality to sink in.

Luke looked about the school grounds, curious if anyone had witnessed his moment of glory. There was no one in sight, but one other person had seen everything.

At first, Luke intended to head straight for Barnes' Sports Store to have a meeting with Jerome. But after his kiss with

Cecilia, the rest of the day passed off in a daze. He spent the whole afternoon sitting on Dun Laoghaire harbour wall, watching the boats come and go, the Stena Seacat setting out on its journey to Holyhead.

Luke couldn't stop himself from smiling. He felt stupid, but happy. It was twenty past seven in the evening and pelting with rain when he reached the front door of 18 Sycamore Street. He rang the doorbell. Isaac answered it, eventually.

'She's out back,' he said.

'Is your dad in?' Luke replied.

Isaac stared at him in confusion for a second, then he clicked his fingers.

'Oh right. You're the next Ryan Giggs,' he said.

Isaac stepped back into the hallway. Luke followed him, but he felt like leaving the Barnes household that instant on principal. *The next Ryan Giggs?* What a cheek. If there was one Man Utd player Luke hated more than any other, it had to be Ryan Giggs (David Beckham and Nicky Butt were close behind in joint second place). To be compared to the Welsh wing wizard was an insult of the highest order.

'Next Francis Jeffers,' Luke said defensively.

'What?' Isaac replied.

'Nothing.'

Isaac showed Luke into the living room. Jerome was sitting in a large black leather armchair, holding his bottom lip between thumb and forefinger, staring blankly at *Xena:Warrior Princess* on Sky One.

'Pop,' Isaac said firmly.

He walked out of the living room as Jerome snapped out of his daydream. Luke smiled politely.

'Alright, boss,' he said.

'Luke,' Jerome replied in surprise.

Luke took a seat on the black leather couch next to the living room door. Jerome picked up a bottle of Budweiser lying on the floor next to his armchair and sipped slowly.

'What can I do for you?' he said.

Luke nibbled on his right index fingernail. He pulled his hand away from his mouth as Jerome finished his swig of beer.

'Don't resign,' he said.

Jerome put the bottle back down on the floor. He sat up in the armchair and stretched his arms out wide, yawning. Then he laughed. He glanced over at Luke briefly.

'If only we'd met last September,' Jerome said.

'The season's not over yet,' Luke replied.

Jerome smiled, but he shook his head.

'Doesn't matter now. I rang the league committee today, asked them to withdraw us from Division E.'

Jerome got to his feet and disappeared from the living room through a set of partition doors that led to the kitchen. Luke took the opportunity to examine the picture frames on top of the Sony TV set.

A young Jerome in his Man Utd kit. Then Jerome, Ella, Isaac and a pretty blonde woman, obviously the mother, outside Barnes' Sports Store. A banner hung over the window: *Official Opening*.

Jerome came back into the living room, can of Coke in hand. He noticed Luke looking through the photos.

'I have one with Paul McGrath,' he said.

Luke turned round with a fright. Jerome smiled, handing him the can of Coke.

'Thanks,' Luke said.

He sat back down on the couch while Jerome rooted through a mahogany cabinet on the right-hand side of the fireplace.

Luke opened the can of Coke. Balanced on his thighs was a photograph he'd found of Ella and her mum. They were standing on a beach. It was a recent photo, but Ella looked different. No glasses, her braided hair let loose around her shoulders, a pair of skimpy denim shorts and a white bikini top. She had wonderfully long slender legs and a tiny waist. Two features usually hidden by her dungarees and duffel coat.

Luke felt like saying, 'wow'. But seeing as the only other man in the room was Ella's father, he kept his mouth shut. Jerome finished rooting in the cabinet and climbed to his feet.

'Decent player. But no natural ability on the ball,' he said. 'Not like yours truly.'

Luke took hold of the second picture frame while Jerome slipped into a daydream of former glories. The photograph was taken on a miserable wet day. *The Cliff, 1983* was written in blue biro in the top left-hand corner of the frame. It was definitely Paul McGrath standing next to Jerome in a Man Utd reserve team line-up. Luke was suitably impressed, but he felt as though he was side-stepping the *real* issue of his visit. The Stretford Enders.

'Can I ask you a question, boss?' Luke said quietly.

Jerome heard the call of dull reality plucking him from his daydream. A crucial defensive header from Barnes, clearing Utd lines in the last minute of a European Cup Final. He scooped his bottle of beer from the floor and took a swig.

'Is there a South Dublin League Cup?' Luke said.

Jerome thought about this question momentarily. He nodded his head. Luke smiled.

'When's the first round?' he said.

Jerome scratched his stubbly chin.

'I'll be back in a minute,' he replied.

Jerome left the living room to find his Enders' fixture diary. Meanwhile, Luke sat on the couch sipping his can of Coke triumphantly. He knew the league cup could prove the turning point for the Enders. As it had done for Everton and Howard Kendall in 1984.

Everton were bottom of the first division before their third round league cup match. The toffees managed to squeeze through to the next round and went on a cup run that brought them all the way to the final against Liverpool. They lost the replay 1–0. But they won the FA Cup final 2–0 against Watford, avoided relegation and the next season were league champions. But Howard Kendall, and Jay, always said it was the league cup that turned things in the right direction.

Jerome wandered back into the living room, his head stuck in a black leather diary.

'Erm, Saturday, three weeks,' he said.

With this news, Luke jumped up from the couch like a hundred metres sprinter bursting out of his starting blocks.

'Don't withdraw from the cup. Give me three weeks to find new players,' he said.

'What's the point?' Jerome replied negatively.

Luke stared at him, wearing his cheeky confident grin.

'We can win the league cup, that's the point.'

Jerome broke into a smile. Somehow, Luke's optimistic outlook had transferred to his brain like a signal from a satellite dish. Luke stuck out his right hand, Jerome shook it. The Stretford Enders, or Luke to be precise, had three weeks to turn their horrid season around.

Luke stood in the empty rehearsal room. It seemed the Funky Starfish had taken the night off. He knocked on the door of the repair room. The sound of 'Simply The Best' by Tina Turner wafted through the door. Luke decided to call her name.

'Ella.'

There was a blank moment before the volume on the stereo lowered. Luke waited for the door to open. When it did, he walked straight past Ella into the repair room.

'Excuse me, Ella. Can I come in please?' she said sarcastically.

Luke couldn't reply. He was completely mesmerised by the fabulous sight before him. The Spitfire had at last started to resemble a Spitfire. In the short space of time since they last talked that morning, Ella had assembled the main structure of the plane. She shut the door behind her and roughly nudged him aside.

'It looks great,' he said.

Ella didn't reply, not that she needed to. Luke was more than content to watch in total silence as she went about her job. The neat and tidy manner in which she carried out her work was in complete contrast to her scruffy appearance.

The construction schematic covered the wall in front of them, temporarily taking precedent over the Man City posters. Luke noticed the parts were laid out in small bundles around the model. The parts list was sellotaped to the desk, a red biro mark ticked off various parts on the list.

Luke picked up a small wooden beam with a row of screws attached to the bottom.

'What's this for? I could never figure it out,' he said.

'Put it down,' Ella replied angrily.

Luke stared at her for a while, then gently replaced the beam to the desk. Ella sighed in frustration, she turned away from him.

'Just leave me to it,' she said.

Luke stood there for a moment.

'Do you want me to go?' he said softly.

Ella didn't bother to reply. Silence was the best way to say yes. Luke nodded his head. He opened the door to leave.

'I'll see you in school.'

Yet again, Ella made no effort to reply.

Luke left Sycamore Street at eight o'clock on the dot. He walked down Harbour Road trying to work out Ella's drastic change in mood. The only sensible explanation he could think of was her time of the month. Martina turned into a monster when she had hers, but Luke knew when it was coming and had the sense to stay clear.

Saturday evening was fast turning to night. It had been another eventful day, but it wasn't over yet.

Montague Avenue was a welcome sight for Luke. He threw an empty packet of smoky bacon Frisps into a blue Corporation bin on the pavement and dug around inside his tracksuit pocket for his front door key.

When Luke came inside, he noticed Mrs Hendy moving about the kitchen through the ajar door. He walked down the hall to say hello.

'Alright, Mrs H,' he said, standing by the kitchen door.

Mrs Hendy was standing at the sink, the taps running. She turned to Luke, wearing a smile.

'How did the match go?' she said.

'I scored two goals. But we got beaten seven-three.'

Luke sat down at the kitchen table. Mrs Hendy turned off the taps, took two tall glasses from a cupboard above the sink and walked over to the fridge. She took out a carton of orange juice and poured two tall glasses.

'How's your friend, Ella was it?' Mrs Hendy said.

She brought the glasses over to the kitchen table. Luke sunk half of his in one go.

'She's alright, I suppose,' he said vaguely.

Luke stared into his glass, swirling the remaining orange

juice around to form a mini whirlpool. He leaned forward and asked a question.

'You know women . . .'

Mrs Hendy's eyes sharpened like an eagle spotting a lame pigeon in trouble on the ground.

'Yes,' she replied.

Luke sat up straight. He rubbed the back of his neck with his right hand. He coughed to kill a bit of time, still trying to work out a way to phrase his question.

'Why are they so moody?' he said.

Luke made his way along the first floor landing. Mrs Hendy had proven no help with his question. She made no attempt to answer, she just started laughing, rustled his hair and walked into her back parlour.

Luke stuck his key in the front door just as Martina opened the lock from the inside. Ronald was standing beside her, turned out in another shocking outfit. Dark orange corduroy trousers and a chequered short-sleeve shirt that belonged on a table in a café.

Martina was wearing her long silver silk skirt, the good one. Her fancy suede high-heel shoes with the straps and a new, tight-fitting grey sweater.

'Where are you going?' Luke said rudely.

Martina was disgusted by the tone of his voice and the impolite nature of his question. She gave Ronald a helpful nudge out the door.

'We're meeting Amanda for a drink,' she replied firmly.

Ronald wore his trademark apologetic grin as Martina shoved him past Luke. They walked down the staircase hand in hand. It caused Luke to sigh in disgust. Ronald wasn't a gold-digger, a dangerous womaniser or a con-man. He was just a prat, plain and simple. Martina could do a lot better.

'When will you be home?' Luke said, shouting down the staircase.

'Late,' Martina replied abruptly.

'What's for tea?'

There was no reply. Luke heard the front door slam shut. He couldn't believe it.

'Ma,' he said loudly, desperately.

Luke was all alone in the hallway. Abandoned, hungry, unloved. Finally, he found the strength to make it inside the front door. The table was laid, Martina had left a two litre bottle of orange Fanta and a jumbo packet of Rancheros. That was for starters, or dessert. There was also a video from Xtra-vision, *The Story of France 98*. And a massive bar of Mint Aero chocolate.

'Nothing but junk food,' Luke said sadly, trying to sound unloved and mistreated.

He opened the door of the microwave to find his dinner sitting there, covered in cellophane. Peas, roast potatoes, stuffing and two large breasts of chicken. Luke set the microwave for three-minutes reheat, then went over to the kitchen table and clicked on the Packard Bell PC to load up the game Ronald had left as a present.

'What a lick-arse,' Luke said as he read the instructions to *Star Wars: Shadows of the Empire*.

Rebuilding the Enders

Luke stood on the touchline of the football pitch at ten to nine on Monday morning. Copper, David Swayne, Alan Giles, the Burke brothers and Edgar stood round him in a semi-circle. David had already broken the news that his brother's walk-out was permanent. Apparently Peter Swayne and Co had signed up for Dalkey United on Sunday morning. It was the best piece of news Luke had heard in weeks.

'OK. We have three weeks until our first round match,' he said.

'What?' Copper replied.

The other boys looked at one another in confusion. Luke nodded his head positively. 'We need four new players,' he said.

'But Mr Barnes resigned,' David replied.

'I talked him round. We made a deal. If I can find four new players, we can play in the League Cup.'

Everyone was silent. But it wasn't a down-hearted silence. Quite the opposite. The remaining Stretford Enders were smiling. It seemed Luke's optimistic outlook on things was catching like the common cold.

'The main problem with this team has gone to Dalkey United,' Luke said. He took a moment before looking over at David. 'No offence.'

'None taken,' David replied.

Luke handed each player a sheet of white paper. It was stage one of his master plan. The outline of a team.

The Stretford Enders

1.
Alan Giles

4.
David Swayne

2.
Muffin Burke

5.
Copper Martin

6.
Edgar O'Lone

3.
Éclair Burke

7.
?

10.
?

8.
?

11.
?

9.
Luke Farrell (c)

The team-sheet was a sight that brought a smile to the Burke brothers. They had spent the entire season on the touchline as substitutes. Luke had watched them play in the daily lunch-time matches. They were tidy players: could pass, tackle, and control the ball. Their only problem would be fitness. But Luke was confident he could make them part of a winning team.

He wasn't so sure about Edgar. He was so small and skinny. A gentle breeze could knock him over. Where would he play?

'I'm a centre-half?' Edgar said happily.

'Well . . . for the time being,' Luke replied awkwardly.

The other boys studied the team-sheet. It still looked rather bare without Swayne and Co, but Luke was right. This was a chance to forge team spirit.

Luke knew better than anyone that teamwork was the only way to be successful. Rathdale Athletic had lots of talented, skilful players. But the secret of their success lay in the simple fact that they always played together, as a team.

'Where will we get players from?' Alan said.

'That's where I'll need some help. I have one possible for centre-midfield, but I need your help to find some wingers. Kids with genuine pace,' Luke replied.

There was a moment of thoughtful silence amongst the group. Everyone seemed to be thinking where they could find two speedy wingers. Finally, David Swayne looked up at Luke from his team-sheet. He was smiling.

'I know *exactly* where to find them,' he said.

The morning meeting came to an end with Alan and Luke arranging to meet David outside the school gates at half twelve the same day. As they walked along the driveway, Alan gave Luke some advice about his twin sister.

'Avoid talking about *Star Search 2000*,' he said.

'What?' Luke replied.

Alan smiled, then tipped his nose with his left index finger. Luke tried to crowbar an explanation from him, but Alan remained tight-lipped.

This was a real problem for Luke. Football had quickly reclaimed a position of priority over romance since Saturday morning. But thanks to this cryptic comment from Alan, the pressure was mounting on him to do something about Cecilia. Was it just a kiss? Or did it mean more?

David was waiting at the school gates as the lads approached.

'Where are we going?' Alan said.

'Running,' David replied.

Alan and Luke followed David all the way across the upper-class housing estates of Foxrock and Stillorgan, without lunch, to reach the athletics track at Oakley Secondary School.

Oakley was nothing like Woodlawn Comprehensive. The main school building was red-brick, old-fashioned, dignified, and the students, who were all boys, wore a neat uniform: navy trousers, black jumper, white shirt and emerald green tie.

David, Alan and Luke took their seats in the stadium grandstand to watch the practice.

'Keep an eye on the kid in lane two,' David said quietly.

A hundred metres sprint was about to begin. The starter fired a gun into the air and the runners took off. Luke and Alan watched as the sprinter in lane two, a tall kid with a lean, muscular build and a head shaped like a peroxide-blond concrete block, raced into an early lead. David glanced at Luke's face, he smiled and said, 'Is that fast enough for you?'

Luke nodded his head, but remained silent.

'Who is he?' Alan said.

'He's my cousin. Leslie Ward, South Dublin under-fourteen sprint champion at one and two hundred metres,' David replied proudly.

Luke looked at David with an expression of uncertainty.

'Leslie? Is that a boy's name?' he said.

David took Alan and Luke beneath the stadium grandstand to the dressing rooms. They walked through a crowd of boys changing back into their school uniforms. Steam drifted out of the shower room in a smoky vapour trail.

'Alright, Les,' David said.

Leslie turned and smiled. He suspended the knot-tying process on his school tie to come over and say hello. He was still wearing his white running shorts and Adidas spike trainers.

'What's the story?' Leslie said as he patted David's shoulder.

'Les, these are friends of mine. Luke and Alan.'

Leslie shook hands with the boys and exchanged polite hellos. It seemed a waste of time to Luke. A top-notch athletics champion with a bright future would hardly jump at the chance to join the worst football team in Dublin.

'So, when do we start training?' Leslie said.

'You want to join?' Luke replied in astonishment.

Leslie smiled and nodded his head positively.

'Can't wait.'

Luke and Alan looked at one another, then David. Everyone was smiling.

'Oh, but I told Lofty as well. Is it OK if he comes along?' Leslie said.

'Who's Lofty?' Luke replied.

The boys left Oakley Secondary School with smiles as wide as the Stillorgan dual carriageway. In one scouting mission they had signed up Leslie Ward and Lofty O'Keefe. Both had represented Dublin and Leinster at Athletics. Leslie could run a hundred metres in under twelve seconds flat while Lofty was South Dublin cross-country champion two years on the trot.

'Two down, two to go,' Luke said as the boys walked down Woodlawn Drive.

The resurrection of the Stretford Enders was well underway. Swayne and Co were unaware of this fact as they called out to Luke from the cover of the bike-shed.

'Hey, Honchee. I hear Knacker FC are looking for players,' Swayne said.

Co laughed out loud, congratulating Swayne on another classic putdown. Luke whispered in David's left ear. He spoke with an Italian gangster accent, like Robert De Niro in the movie *Goodfellas*.

'Funny guy.'

It sent David into fits of laughter. Swayne and Co couldn't

hear the joke. They stopped laughing, their faces frozen in a stare of paranoia.

'Say it out loud, Honchee,' Swayne said, shouting.

Luke, David and Alan ignored Swayne and Co and walked on towards the main building, smiling. This was the first victory Luke had managed over Swayne and Co without the use of a football. Things were on the up and up for the Stretford Enders.

Training

Luke stood outside the school gates, which were locked for the evening. Copper, Alan, the Burke brothers and Edgar stood before him, decked out in tracksuits and trainers. The last people to arrive were David, Leslie and Lofty O'Keefe.

'Luke, this is Lofty,' David said, introducing the Enders' newest recruit.

Lofty deserved his nickname. He was well over six foot tall. He nodded his head shyly to the rest of the group. Lofty had curly brown hair, a chin to rival Jimmy Hill's and large buck teeth. He reminded Luke of Chris Waddle from his physical appearance, lean and lanky. If he could play anything like Waddle, Luke would be very happy.

'Thanks for coming along, lads,' Luke said.

He had been cooking an inspirational speech in his head the whole day. But seeing as they were still two players short of a full eleven, he decided to hold onto it for another occasion.

'The game against St David's. Two main problems. We're going to deal with the first one tonight. Fitness,' Luke said.

The Enders looked at one another. Muffin and Éclair gulped nervously. The words 'fitness' and 'lack of' affected them the most. They would suffer most under Luke's new regime.

'To play for seventy minutes we need to be physically fit.

So, from now on, we meet here each night at seven o'clock for a five-mile run,' he said.

The Burke brothers almost fainted on the spot. It inspired muttered conversations amongst the other Enders. Leslie and Lofty entered into their own whispered conference. David asked them to join a football team. The prospect of a five-mile run each evening made them nervous.

'I thought this was a football team,' Leslie said in protest.

'It is, but not everyone has your level of fitness,' Luke replied, winning over his new recruits with some good old fashioned praise.

'You'll play plenty of football. But I need your help to raise our fitness level,' he said, heaping the adulation on with a shovel.

It worked a treat. Leslie and Lofty were blushing with embarrassment.

'OK, lads, let's do some stretches,' Leslie said, clapping his hands together enthusiastically.

Luke joined in with the other boys as Leslie took them through a simple warm-up routine to prevent injury. The Enders began their five-mile run at a steady jogging pace. Lofty led the way. He mapped out the regular course for the five-mile runs as they went along.

The route he chose went round the school grounds, down Sycamore Street, up past Harbour Road, out onto Woodlawn Park and back to the school gates. Luke, Copper and David coped well with the pace set by Lofty. Edgar, Alan and the Burke brothers felt the pain.

'I'm a goalkeeper. Why do I need to run?' Alan said, in between gasps for air.

The sight of the school gates started to resemble a mirage in the desert, too good to be true. The four back markers crossed over the road from the park to Woodlawn Drive and collapsed in one large heap of sweat on the pavement outside the gates.

'What do you think you're doing?' Leslie said angrily.

The boys looked up at him, gasping like a horde of asthmatic donkeys. Leslie pointed round the school grounds.

'Last lap,' he said firmly.

'What?' Muffin Burke replied in breathless despair.

Leslie stood waiting. He wore a humourless expression and was in no mood to show his team-mates any mercy. Somehow, the four Enders helped one another to their feet and struggled onwards.

Luke, Copper, David and Lofty were already well into their last lap by this time. Luke knew that David and Copper were physically fit. But to play the tactics he had dreamed up for the Stretford Enders, everyone would need to be super-fit. Thankfully, that wasn't a problem with Leslie and Lofty.

'Lofty, are you keeping times?' Luke said.

Lofty, who acted as a pacemaker for the lead group, nodded his head. He had a Seiko stop-watch strapped round his neck. The case in which he covered the five miles, without really breaking into a sweat, was encouraging.

With Lofty and Leslie on the wings, the Enders would have genuine pace to counter-attack. This would be important. Luke was soaked in optimism, but he knew the reality of the situation. The Enders would spend most of their time defending, even in home matches.

'Last stretch, lads. Let's try and lift it,' Lofty said.

Luke, Copper and David responded. As they raised their pace to a sprint across Woodlawn Park, Luke caught sight of some small boys kicking a ball about behind the burnt out Nissan Micra.

One in particular caught his eye. Small and skinny, he kept

the ball under sublime control, as if he had a magnet hidden inside his left shoe. The other boys chased after him like a pack of hungry dogs fighting over a bone.

Luke let Copper and David pass him by, he couldn't help but come to a halt. The kickabout involved thirteen or fourteen lads, jumpers for goal-posts. They were small kids, no more than ten or eleven years of age. But one boy played beyond age.

'Close him down,' the goalkeeper shouted.

The opposing team surrounded the boy on every side. But somehow he managed to zigzag his way through swiping tackles and shoulder-charges with the elegance and grace of a ballet dancer. Such balance and skill. The ball seemed to be glued to his left foot. Luke started urging the boy on quietly.

'Go on,' he said to himself.

The boy switched direction on his marker with a majestic Cruyff flick. It left him in on goal. The keeper skidded out, feet first, trying to smother the ball. But the kid chipped it over him with a nonchalant flick of his left foot. Luke laughed at the audacity. He started clapping. The other boys left for home, it seemed they were playing the old 'next goal the winner' rule. And what a winning goal.

'Here, kid,' Luke said, shouting.

He ran onto the pitch to talk with the boy.

'Great goal,' he said.

The boy looked at Luke in confusion. He had dark brown hair, striking features and olive-coloured skin. Luke took a quick glance at his feet. The boy had played the match wearing tattered brown leather shoes.

'Great goal,' Luke said slowly.

The boy smiled blankly. He shook his head and raised his hands. He was trying to signal that he couldn't understand.

'He doesn't speak English,' a voice said.

Luke turned round. Another boy with the same coloured skin and hair, except taller, stood in front of him.

'Are you brothers?' Luke said.

The boy was reluctant to answer.

'I play for a football team. I'm looking for new players,' Luke said.

The boy stared at Luke with a sense of fear and mistrust. The little boy said something to his brother in a foreign language. He pointed at Luke. The older boy started talking.

'My name is Daniel. This is my brother, Ille.'

Luke smiled, he reached out his right hand towards Daniel. 'I'm Luke,' he said.

'I have been in Ireland a year with my mother. Ille and my father arrived only two months ago.'

' . . . that's why he can't speak any English?' Luke cut in.

Daniel nodded. Luke turned to shake Ille's hand. The brothers had a short conference in their foreign language. Obviously the discussion was to do with Luke and his intentions. Daniel tipped Luke's left shoulder.

'Ille wants to play. But he has no football shoes.'

Luke smiled, he turned and shook hands with Ille. 'We meet outside the school gates. Tomorrow, seven o'clock,' he said.

'What about the shoes?' Daniel replied.

Luke turned to face Daniel. It was funny, Ille wasn't more than ten or eleven years of age. But already he had his big brother acting as his agent, looking after his football career.

'I'll sort something out,' Luke said.

Daniel and Ille watched as Luke ran off towards the school gates. The back markers were coming into Woodlawn Park as he started to run again.

The sight of the great Luke Farrell barely beating them to the finish line was an uplifting sight, it spurred the boys on to a desperate sprint. The back markers found new energy in their tired legs and crossed the finish line in under the fifty minute mark.

The Enders stood outside the school gates, panting heavily. Lofty and Leslie looked as fresh as daisies. They were in conference about the lap times. David and Copper looked over at Luke.

'What happened to you?' Copper said.

Luke was hunched on his knees, taking deep breaths. He smiled at the lads, stood upright, and walked off down Woodlawn Drive, urging them to follow with a wave of his right hand.

'I'll tell you outside Kelly's,' Luke replied.

The Enders sat on the wooden benches outside Kelly's newsagents, sipping their bottles of Lucozade Sport in between their laboured attempts to scoff down bananas. Luke had his trusty team-sheet out, pencilling in a new name.

'I saw this kid in the park,' he said quietly.

A moment of silent contemplation led Copper to interrupt with a question.

'What's he like?'

Luke tapped the butt of the pencil against Ille's name on the team-sheet.

'A mini-Maradona,' he said.

THE FINAL PIECE IN THE JIGSAW

Monday night was a complete success. On the way back to Montague Avenue, Luke had a quiet word with Muffin and Éclair Burke about a new low-calorie diet he wanted them to stick too.

The Burke brothers had gained their nicknames from their favourite cakes. It wasn't really their fault, their mother was the owner of the Burke Family Bakery. A successful business with fourteen shops across South Dublin. But to play at full-back, the brothers needed to shed a stone each. Again, Luke employed some of his expert man-management motivational skills.

'Take a look at this,' he said.

He handed Muffin a football programme. Rathdale Athletic vs Home Farm. The Dublin Schoolboy U-13 Cup Final, May 15th 1999.

'Turn to page ten,' Luke said.

Muffin turned to page ten. Éclair leaned in for a closer look as Luke pointed to two faces in the Rathdale Athletic team photo.

'Robbie Molloy plays at right-back. Luton, Blackburn and Sunderland have sent scouts to watch him play. Derek Fisher plays at left-back. Nottingham Forest, West Ham and Liverpool want to take him on trial. If you stick to this diet for three weeks, I won't ask them to join the Stretford Enders.'

It was cruel, threatening to snatch away their dreams of first-team football. But Luke sensed that a 'tough love' policy would work for the Burke brothers. If they were assured of their places either way, the temptation for the odd cream doughnut would become too much to resist.

'Robbie and Derek are good mates. I'd have no trouble getting them to sign for the Enders. But I don't want to. I've watched you play in the lunch-time games. You're good players. Lose a little weight and you'll be great players,' Luke said.

Even as the words left his mouth he could see their spirits rise. It was exactly what they needed. A goal to aim towards.

'Deal,' Muffin said, offering Luke his hand.

Luke shook hands with the Burke brothers. He held up his left thumb as a sign of goodbye before turning onto Montague Avenue. The sight of the Burke brothers heading back up Harbour Road, locked in an excited debate about the challenge ahead, gave him a warm feeling inside. The only downside he faced on Monday night was the childish giggles of Martina and Ronald.

They were in the living room, watching some stupid video, *Monty Python and The Holy Grail*. Luke was in his bedroom, trying to work out a training schedule for the footballing side of things. But he found it impossible to concentrate.

Ronald kept shouting 'Ni,' in a high pitched voice. It was in reference to some silly joke from the movie. Luke felt like punching him in the face. But worse than Ronald shouting 'Ni' every ten seconds was Martina. She was giggling at him like some ten-year-old schoolgirl. Luke knew Martina, she didn't laugh at things like Monty Python, not until she met Ronald.

'Could you turn it down?' Luke said in protest.

Martina stared at him. He stood outside his bedroom door

wearing only his Everton boxer shorts. Ronald tried to plug up the tense silence with an apology.

'Yes, of course, Luke. I'm very sorry.'

This remark infuriated Martina. She nudged Ronald in the ribs with her right elbow. He started to panic, yet again he was dumped in the middle of a mother-son warzone. Like all good diplomats, Ronald tried to offer a compromise to keep everyone happy.

'Would you like to join us, Luke?'

The resounding slam of his bedroom door represented an obvious no. The volume on the TV dropped down a notch or three, not that it made Luke any happier. Instead, he went back to his team-sheet, trying to shut out the outside world, or more precisely, the living room.

On Tuesday morning, Luke felt a lot better about things. He left for school at half-eight, hoping to enlist the help of his goalkeeper on a very special scouting mission. This was a vital signing that would complete his team-sheet.

'Alan,' Luke said.

2C were leaving Miss Court's English class. Luke detained Alan for a private chat. Miss Court ushered them both outside of room fourteen.

'What do you know about Tonka Matthews?' Luke said.

Alan looked him straight in the eyes. 'He's a nutter. That's all you need to know,' he replied.

'Why?'

Luke remained silent, gripping the straps on his schoolbag anxiously. Alan looked at him, hoping beyond hope it wasn't what he thought it was.

'No,' he said fearfully.

Luke shrugged his shoulders.

'The one thing this team lacks is a nutter,' he replied.

*

It took Luke twenty minutes to talk Alan into helping him. They walked down Harbour Road that afternoon, carefully scanning the houses on both sides of the road for a front garden full of tombstones. This was the best landmark Copper Martin had been able to give them for identifying Tonka Matthews' house. When Luke invited Copper to join the scouting mission as chief navigator he'd refused immediately, offering a very suspect excuse.

'Dentist appointment me arse,' Alan said with a bitter snarl.

Luke walked ahead of Alan. He searched the gardens on the left side of Harbour Road for a sign of tombstones piled high.

'Alan,' he said quietly.

He tugged on the sleeve of Alan's navy Russell Athletic jumper. Alan turned to look in the same direction as Luke. They both stared across Harbour Road at a garden, stocked high with marble tombstones. White, black, green, lots of different colours.

'There it is,' Luke said, gulping nervously.

'Yeah,' Alan replied.

It would be very easy to back out now. After all, there had to be plenty of nutters living about Dun Laoghaire. Surely one of them would like to play centre-midfield for the Stretford Enders.

'Come on,' Luke said, grabbing hold of Alan's right arm.

They waited for a 46A bus to zoom by before crossing over Harbour Road. Luke walked ahead of Alan into the garden. The front door was wide open. The sound of an electric saw grinding through marble emanated from inside the house. This horrific screeching sound was more than enough for Alan Giles. He tried to break free, save himself from becoming the victim of a chainsaw massacre.

'Alan,' Luke said, shouting.

He stood alone in the garden, watching Alan Giles sprint up Harbour Road like Linford Christie. Luke shook his head in disgust.

'He wasn't running that fast last night,' he said bitterly.

It was only now he noticed the massive shadow, bearing down on him like a UFO hovering overhead. Luke turned around slowly. He stood face to face with Tonka Matthews, who wore an unearthly frown.

'What do you want?' he said, almost growling.

Luke stood his ground. This wasn't a moment to show fear, it was a moment to show strength and bravery. 'Say something,' he screamed to himself. Tonka was growing impatient, some kind of blunt (or sharp) instrument would soon be heading toward his skull. It was a stupid thing to say, but Luke said it anyway.

'Can I come in?'

Tonka looked at him, his upper lip on the edge of a vicious snarl. Luke chewed his bottom lip in despair. This was a bad idea.

But then, to his complete astonishment, Tonka stood aside, inviting Luke to walk into the hall. He locked the front door after them, shutting out any possible chance of escape. But Luke held his nerve.

He followed the man mountain up the staircase. The next problem he faced was asking him to join the Enders. 'What a stupid idea,' Luke cried to himself. It wasn't as if Tonka Matthews even liked football.

Luke walked into Tonka's bedroom. 'No way,' he said in amazement. It was a shrine to the super toffees. Well, the toffees on the left side of the room, Megadeath, Slayer, Soundgarden and the giants of rock and heavy metal on the right side.

Luke headed straight for an FA Cup final programme lying

on Tonka's bed. It was from 1995, the glorious 1–0 victory over the scum of Man Utd.

'What's this about?' Tonka said.

Luke turned round. He had lost the plot for a moment. The excitement of finding a fellow Evertonian in Dun Laoghaire. He took a moment to compose himself, but he no longer felt nervous.

'Can you play football?' Luke said.

It didn't look like Tonka was going to answer him. He stared straight through Luke. His face was like a stone statue, no expression, happy or sad.

'Why?' he replied, finally.

'I need a centre-midfielder. Someone to win the ball.'

Tonka walked across to his bedroom window. He opened it a little, letting in a breath of fresh sea air.

'You don't think I can pass the ball?' he said softly.

'What do you mean?' Luke replied.

Tonka sat on his bed. He pulled a blue Everton jersey from beneath his pillows.

'That's all I've ever got. Win the ball, kick people, put yourself about. I can do more than that,' he said.

Tonka removed his Iron Maiden T-shirt, revealing a muscular physique. He replaced the T-shirt with his Everton jersey. As he did so, Luke spotted a photograph stuck beneath the frame of the mirror on his wardrobe.

Tonka was decked out in a wine-coloured football kit, standing in the back row of a team line-up. His long hair was tied in a ponytail. His team-mates were tall lads, they looked about eighteen years old.

'I found this kid last night who plays like Maradona. I want to play him as an attacking midfielder. But he's only eleven. He'll get crushed. Come to think of it, the whole team will get crushed,' Luke said.

Tonka looked at him. It was time to shovel some praise on the fire.

'I need a Peter Reid. A leader.'

It was a good start, but Tonka still looked undecided. Luke came back with the clinching line.

'We've no chance without you.'

Luke left Harbour Road in a state of unbridled bliss. His team-sheet was complete, The Stretford Enders were back from the dead. Now all he had to do was mould them into a unit. Tuesday evening was the perfect time for that inspirational speech and explanation of how the new look Stretford Enders would line up.

It was a heart-warming sight for Luke. The heavy rain shower and gusty breeze had done nothing to dilute the enthusiasm for the team. Five to seven on Tuesday evening. Ten players standing before him, all ready to work their socks off.

'Lads, take one each,' Luke said.

He passed out photocopies of the completed team-sheet.

'This is how we line out,' he said.

The Stretford Enders

1.
Alan Giles

4.
David Swayne

2.	5.	6.	3.
Muffin Burke	Edgar O'Lone	Copper Martin	Éclair Burke

7.	8.	10.	11.
Leslie Ward	Ille Popsecu	Tonka Matthews	Lofty O'Keefe

9.
Luke Farrell (c)

'David will play as sweeper. So it's a basic 5–4–1 formation,' Luke said.

Ille whispered to Daniel in Romanian. He kept pointing to Tonka's name on the team-sheet. Daniel looked about the players. He pointed him out to Ille. He and Tonka shared a momentary glance. Ille muttered something to Daniel, then smiled at Tonka. A smile of fear.

'Farrell,' Tonka said.

Luke walked over to his side.

'This kid plays like Maradona?' he said cynically.

'Maybe even better,' Luke replied confidently.

He tapped his right fist against Tonka's bulging bicep. Almost immediately, Luke regretted this overly friendly physical sign of affection. They stared at one another. For a brief, but terrifying, moment. It seemed like Tonka was about to chin him.

'OK, Les. Let's get going,' Luke said nervously, desperate to move out of range of Tonka's fists.

The Enders went off on their five-mile run. Leslie took the lead group, consisting of Luke, David, Copper and Tonka. Lofty brought up the rear with the Burke brothers, Edgar, Alan and Ille. Although it was only the second night of the five-mile run, everyone completed the course in a time below forty five minutes. As the boys stood on the school driveway, hands on knees, breathing heavily, Luke broke the silence.

'Kelly's,' he said.

The Enders were queuing along the counter in Kelly's newsagents, deep in discussion about the challenge ahead. Luke noticed Ille and Daniel standing outside. Everyone else had the money to buy drinks, Ille and Daniel obviously did not.

Luke kept quiet about this fact. He used up the rest of his pocket money to buy Ille and Daniel bottles of Lucozade

Sport and a banana each. He told them it was courtesy of the Stretford Enders, in an attempt to save their feelings.

Luke smiled at Ille. He had settled into the training programme effortlessly. He seemed quite happy to run for five miles, even though he couldn't understand a word anyone around him said. As night fell on Woodlawn Drive, Luke stood beneath the orange glare of a street-lamp to conduct his speech.

'Football is two things. Defending, and attacking. When we have the ball, no matter where on the pitch, we're attacking. When we don't have the ball, we're defending. It's that simple.'

Luke gave his pearl of wisdom a moment to breathe. It took Daniel a few seconds longer to translate the speech into Romanian for Ille. Everyone seemed happy with the new formation and strategy. No one commented on his philosophical definition of football.

'Les and Lofty give us pace on the wings. Tonka gives us strength and leadership in the middle. Ille gives us that little something special,' Luke said.

Ille smiled when Daniel finished translating. Luke moved across to the members of his back five. He slung his arms round Edgar and Copper's shoulders. Edgar was busy taking a gasp of his inhaler.

'The back five have to be strong. Let's face it, you're gonna be under some amount of pressure. But it's a team game. The whole point of defending and attacking is this . . .'

Luke left a dramatic pause. It was startling how effective his teamtalk had been so far. Everyone, even Tonka, dangled in mid-air, awaiting his next word.

' . . . We defend as a team. Attack as a team,' he said quietly.

Time for another of those trusty pauses, just to add a little thinking time for the Enders. Ille nodded his head in agreement, Tonka seemed impressed, Leslie and Lofty had no idea what Luke was talking about, but they nodded their heads in a positive fashion.

'The only way we can win, is as a team.'

What a way to finish an evening's work. It left everyone in a state of awe and wonder. Luke walked down Harbour Road with Tonka and the Burke brothers, certain that the long journey down the road to footballing glory had begun.

'See you, Farrell,' Tonka said as he turned into his front garden.

Luke waved his right hand in reply.

It was a scary sight. But he was certain he saw Tonka Matthews smile.

KILLING THE HAMMERHEAD

Jerome stood on the touchline, watching his new-look team complete their second lap of the pitch. Four new faces, not to mention the Romanian kid's brother/agent/translator. And what had happened to the Burke brothers? Starvation diet no doubt. They must have lost over a stone each.

'Luke,' Jerome said.

Luke broke off from the pack as the Enders went into their third lap of the pitch, he took a deep breath while Jerome prepared his list of questions.

'Who have we got here?' he said, scratching behind his left ear in confusion.

'Tonka and Ille. They play centre-midfield. Leslie and Lofty. Right and left wing,' Luke replied.

Jerome nodded his head. Luke smiled, confident about his new team-mates. They had worked hard over the last sixteen days. Each Ender had run an aggregate of eighty miles in an effort to raise their fitness level. It was working. Leslie gave a shout on the far side of the pitch.

'Lift it,' he said.

Jerome watched closely as the Enders broke into a sprint as a unit. The group stayed together, even the Burke brothers and Edgar managing to keep pace with the rest. As they passed by Jerome on the touchline, Luke rejoined the group.

'OK. Last lap,' Jerome said, shouting after them.

He removed a stick of Juicy Fruit chewing gum from its wrapper. He was already chewing when it occurred to him.

'Gum?' he said politely.

'Thank you,' Daniel replied, removing a stick from the half-full packet.

On the far side of the pitch, Copper and David were having a quiet word in Luke's ear.

'He won't go for it,' Copper said firmly.

'He will,' Luke replied.

Copper and David were concerned about Jerome's input on team tactics. It could mean the Stretford Enders returning to the dreaded hammerhead formation. Luke was determined to prevent such a tactical blunder. Again, he would rely on his blossoming man-management skills, this time laying the praise on the manager.

'OK, lads. I think it's time to talk tactics,' Jerome said as the boys ground to a halt around him.

Copper and David groaned quietly. But Luke was alive to the danger.

'How about a five-a-side, boss?' he said.

Jerome looked his way, he seemed indifferent to the idea.

'You probably want to see the lads in action.'

Luke crossed his fingers behind his back. Jerome nodded his head slightly, he seemed to be warming to the idea. He threw the football towards Luke's chest.

'Pick teams.'

The boys drifted into the centre-circle. Luke whispered to his team-mates quietly. 'Leave this to me.'

Luke sat out the five-a-side to work on Jerome. They stood on the touchline watching the lads kick-off. Unfortunately, the action on the pitch interrupted Luke's attempt to manipulate Jerome into discarding the dreaded hammerhead formation. It also brought to light a few problems Luke hadn't anticipated.

'What the . . .' Jerome said in despair.

David Swayne glanced at the touchline briefly. He shrugged his shoulders in shame. Luke sighed quietly, tossing his eyes towards the heavens.

Leslie Ward and Lofty O'Keefe, two of the 'star signings', were actually the worst footballers in the history of football. It took fifteen minutes for either of them to touch the ball without falling over.

Luke had always been suspicious. It just seemed too good to be true. Two top-rate athletes eager to sign on for a Division E football team. Now it made more sense. What David Swayne had neglected to tell Luke about Leslie and Lofty was the reason they concentrated on athletics. They couldn't kick snow off a rope.

Jerome's jaw was almost dragging along the muddy floor as he watched in shattered disbelief. Luke cringed as Leslie tried to tackle Copper on the halfway line. Copper nutmegged Leslie who proceeded to slip onto his arse like Bambi on an ice-rink.

'These are the new signings,' Jerome said calmly.

'Erm . . . yeah,' Luke replied.

Jerome stared at Luke. He didn't say a single word but it was obvious he wanted an explanation. It was time to get Jerome's focus back on the positives.

'Give it to Ille,' Luke said, shouting.

His instruction reached Alan just as he was going to fling the ball to Muffin Burke. He abandoned that idea and picked out Ille instead. The little wizard collected the ball outside the penalty area. He proceeded to weave through five tackles until Tonka toe-poked the ball to safety outside the penalty area. Jerome's face brightened a bit.

'It's like you said, boss. The midfield was lacking pace, power and a bit of something special,' Luke said.

He put his right hand out in front of his chest, palm towards the sky.

'There you go. Pace, power and something very special.'

Luke had put his cards on the table. Jerome watched the action quietly, he started nodding his head.

'Can you teach those wingers to kick a ball and chase after it?' Jerome said.

'No problem,' Luke replied.

They smiled at one another. Out on the pitch, Ille saved the day with another piece of individual brilliance. He skipped past four players before shooting wide from an acute angle. Tonka tipped Ille on the shoulder, he shouted across at Daniel.

'Tell him to pass it now and again.'

Daniel nodded his head. He shouted the translation back to Ille, who nodded his head to Tonka in agreement.

Tonka patted Ille on the back.

'What's he wearing?' Jerome said.

He caught sight of Ille's boots. Luke had promised to sort something out. The best he could do was offer him an old Everton away jersey, a pair of black Umbro shorts and his illuminous Lotto boots from last season. The only problem being, the boots were a size six, when Ille took a size four. The solution had been to stuff the toe-ends with newspapers.

'He can't afford boots,' Luke said.

Jerome watched Ille jink past Copper and Edgar inside the penalty area before nutmegging Alan.

Jerome smiled, letting a little laugh of delight escape his mouth. 'Leave that to me,' he said with a broad smile.

Luke had one last matter to deal with, killing the dreaded hammerhead formation.

'It looks good,' he said brightly.

'Yeah,' Jerome replied, keeping his attention on the action.

'Still. We should be realistic.'

This comment drew Jerome's attention like bait on a hook draws a fish.

'What do you mean?' he said.

Luke turned towards Jerome, opened his mouth to answer, paused mid-breath and simply muttered, 'Na.'

Jerome was snapping at the hook now. It was a simple job of reeling him in.

'This is gonna sound. I mean, it's so obvious,' Luke said.

Jerome smiled, trying to divide his attention between Luke and the pitch.

'No, go on,' he said.

Luke saw his chance to land the catch of the day. He took a breath, counted to five, then said it.

'Well. We'd be foolish not to play with a sweeper.'

Jerome thought about it for a moment. Luke timed his follow-up to perfection.

'I mean. Considering how many goals we conceded against St David's, it makes sense to play on the break, with one man up front.'

Luke waited anxiously for Jerome's response. This was it. The revolutionary Farrell 5–4–1 formation or the dreaded hammerhead.

David Swayne muttered something in Copper's right ear, both had watched the conversation on the touchline with great interest.

'Yeah, yeah, of course. Exactly what I planned,' Jerome replied confidently.

Luke had to contain a powerful urge to whoop and cheer in celebration. Jerome folded his arms with a contented grin.

Luke jogged into the centre-circle to join the kickabout. David immediately walked forward to mark him.

'Well?' David said.

'Sorted,' Luke replied.

David whispered yes in delight. He clenched his fist and threw a thumb up to Copper. The news spread like wildfire throughout the rest of the team.

'Oh, one more thing,' Luke said. 'You've got five days to teach our wingers how to kick a football.'

David stood still in the centre-circle as Luke tore away from him with the ball. He watched as Luke dribbled past Lofty, who fell into the mud for the umpteenth time that morning as he tried to make a tackle.

'Fair enough,' David said quietly.

It was Friday. The day before the first round match against Valley Rangers, a team in the top half of Division B of the South Dublin League. Luke walked into the science mall. He spotted Tonka standing alone outside science room three.

Luke smiled, walked across and handed him a match programme from Everton vs Bayern Munich. The second leg of the European Cup Winners' Cup semi-final from April, 1985. Everton smashed the mighty German club 3–0 that night to squeeze through to the final.

Tonka smiled back. He held his thumb aloft then started flicking through the pages of the programme. Luke glanced about the mall. Science was an optional class, so the students of 2C were split between Science, Home Economics and Art.

Cecilia and her gang of followers entered the mall, taking up a position outside home economics room one. Luke waved across to her. She had a clear sight of his salute but casually turned her head and walked on by.

'What's her problem?' Luke said softly.

A few seconds later, Ella strolled into the science mall. He decided to wave at her. Again, Ella noticed his greeting straight away. She stared right back at him, but made no attempt to reply.

Luke heard a gleeful snigger from behind. When he looked round to investigate, Tonka buried his head deep into the pages of the programme and rolled a finger along the volume control of his Walkman.

'Very funny,' Luke said quietly.

Women were funny creatures. Cecilia and Ella were standing a mere fifteen feet away. Yet both acted as if Luke were a complete stranger. It was so stupid. Cecilia kissed *him*, she was the one who ran across the damp grass that Saturday morning. Why was she acting so cold towards him now?

As for Ella. What was her problem? He was keeping his side of the bargain. She had nothing to complain about. Luke kicked his right foot against the wall outside science room three. He had turned his back on women, quite literally.

'Honchee,' Swayne said.

Luke groaned, he swung round slowly to find Swayne and Co standing at the entrance to the science mall, wearing broad grins. Swayne walked forward, stopping two feet away from Luke's face.

'I hear you and the losers have a new team?' Swayne said.

Luke smiled. 'Losers? We can't do much worse than you.'

Swayne was incensed. He grabbed a handful of Luke's jumper and flung him roughly against the wall.

Swayne moved forward to retake his hold of Luke's jumper. He had his right finger poised to act as a prompter while he issued a threatening remark, when a large hand gripped his throat.

Casey came to Swayne's aid. He tried to break Tonka's strangle-hold, but a precise and powerful shove to the chest sent Casey crashing to the floor. Swayne struggled for air, his face was turning purple.

'I'd be careful who you call a loser,' Tonka said.

He allowed Swayne's face to turn a darker shade of purple before removing his giant paw from his neck. Swayne dropped to his knees, coughing and splurting for oxygen. Casey and Co helped their leader back onto his feet, but took great care not to venture too close to Tonka.

Tonka stood on Luke's right side like a bodyguard, awaiting any further comments or acts of violence.

'This isn't over, Honchee,' Swayne said, coughing.

Tonka nudged his clenched fist against Luke's shoulder. It was a gentle nudge, but even that felt like a heavy blow from a lump hammer.

'Nice one,' Luke said.

Cecilia and Ella had been paying attention. But now the fun and games were over, they went back to pretending Luke didn't exist. At this point Mrs James, the Home Economics teacher, and Mr Clarke, the Science teacher, entered the mall together. As they ushered their classes inside, Tonka had a quiet word in Luke's ear.

'I hope we win now.'

Luke nodded in reply.

THE STRETFORD ENDERS
VS
VALLEY RANGERS

Luke arrived at the school grounds for quarter past ten on Saturday morning. The nets were up, the corner flags out and every other Ender was in their kit, ready for kick-off.

'Morning, lads,' Luke said happily as he reached the touchline.

The boys responded with one mass mumble. Nerves were affecting everyone, apart from Tonka and Ille. Tonka was sitting on the touchline, listening to his Walkman, while Ille was talking to Daniel. He was wearing new boots, socks and shorts.

Daniel walked across to Luke, wearing a smile.

'I say thank you to Mr Barnes,' he said.

Luke nodded his head. He patted Daniel on the arm but was busy looking out onto the pitch.

David, Lofty and Leslie were in the centre-circle, passing the ball between each other. Luke noticed the care and attention Leslie took in stopping the ball with his instep, then cleanly side-footing it across to Lofty. David lifted his thumb to Luke, but there was no smile.

Luke sat down between the Burke brothers.

'How much is it now?' he said.

'Sixteen,' Muffin replied.

Éclair was busy reading Edgar's copy of *Fortean Times*. Muffin gave him a helpful tap on the ankle.

'What?' Éclair said.

'Luke was asking how much it is now?'

'Oh, sixteen.'

Luke smiled at Éclair, who went back to reading an article about UFO landings in the outback of Australia. He noticed a bag of apples in his kit bag. Luke used Muffin's left shoulder for leverage to get to his feet.

Jerome was over with the referee, he shook hands with the ref, then walked across and did the same with the Valley Rangers' manager.

'Lads,' Luke said as Jerome walked back towards him.

Tonka, Ille, David, Leslie and Lofty joined the other Enders on the touchline as Jerome prepared his team talk. He threw a stick of Juicy Fruit chewing gum into his mouth before he began.

'The second and third rounds of the cup are to be played this Tuesday and Thursday evening. Just in case we get through.'

That was it. The team talk amounted to a service announcement. The Enders took to the field to face Valley Rangers – a team from Division B, three leagues above them. They were decked out in orange jerseys, shorts and socks. Luke called heads for the coin toss. As the ref spun the 50p piece in the air, Luke noticed the barren wasteland of the touchline.

Valley Rangers had three substitutes and their manager. The Enders had Jerome and Daniel, who gratefully accepted a piece of chewing gum from the Enders manager. No Cecilia, no Ella, it seemed like everyone had deserted him. It was all about football now. Luke smiled at the wonderful thought.

'From the start, Enders,' Tonka said, clapping his hands together to encourage his team-mates, just like Anto Morris, Luke's captain at Rathdale Athletic would do.

Valley Rangers kicked off, it was now or never for the Stretford Enders.

Valley Rangers had been camped in the Enders' penalty area for ten solid minutes.

'Keeper's,' Alan said, screaming.

He threw out a fist to punch the ball away but found fresh air. The ball was about to land on the forehead of the Rangers No.9. At the last moment, David Swayne moved in front of him and glanced it to safety.

'Alan, stay on your line,' he said calmly.

The Enders took a man each as the Rangers No.7 prepared to swing in another corner. The pressure was immense, but the defence had battled bravely. The No.7 knocked a short-corner to the No.10. Lofty stayed tight to his man, who picked up the ball inside the box.

'Stay on your feet, Lofty,' Tonka said.

It was too late. The Rangers No.10 dribbled past Lofty, who panicked and stuck out one of his long gangly legs.

'Ref,' the Rangers manager said, screaming in protest.

Jerome's head dropped in despair as the ref pointed to the spot. Luke went across and lifted Lofty onto his feet.

'Forget about it. Get on with your game,' he said.

Alan Giles stood face to face with the Rangers No.9. You could hear an earwig clear his throat as the No.9 ran forward and whacked the ball with his right foot. It zoomed into the bottom left-hand corner, but Alan flung himself across and got a hand to the ball. Everyone froze in shock.

Everyone except the Rangers No.9 who rushed in to tap

home the rebound . . . Oh, and David Swayne who toe-poked the ball to safety.

'Come on,' Alan said, screaming to his team-mates.

This was it: the turning point. Suddenly, the Enders were winning everything, in the air, on the floor. Luke's insistence on a patient passing style paid dividends. Even Edgar was finding Copper and Éclair Burke with neat, accurate five and ten yard passes. Nothing elaborate, just simple passing.

The game drifted on towards half-time. It was scoreless and the Enders had given as good as they got. Jerome was still subdued in supporting his team, but he watched the action with a renewed hope.

The Rangers goalkeeper kicked the ball, from his hands, towards the centre-circle. Tonka rose high above his marker and flicked it into space on his left. He was having a fantastic game in centre-midfield. He won everything in the air, on the ground. But he wasn't just a workhorse, he was an intelligent footballer.

'Ille,' Tonka said.

His header dropped in front of the little Romanian who was alive to the chance. He charged forward, weaving past tackles from the Rangers No.7 and No.2. He steamed onwards to the edge of the penalty area.

Ille's solo run put the Rangers defence on the back-foot. Luke used the distraction to spin off his marker and dart into a space outside the right-hand side of the penalty area. Ille saw this movement and chipped an exquisite pass over the heads of the defence, it dropped nicely in front of Luke.

'Hit it,' Jerome said quietly.

Luke obliged, smashing the ball on the half-volley. It flew across the goalkeeper, low into the left-hand corner of the net. Jerome started screaming in a high-pitched voice.

'Yessss.'

He and Daniel hugged, then danced a little jig on the touchline. Luke ran across to congratulate Ille, whom Tonka had already trapped in an affectionate headlock. The other Enders sprinted up the pitch to join in with the celebrations, apart from Edgar and the Burke brothers who were too tired from working so hard at the back.

'Come, boys,' Ille said as Rangers prepared to kick-off.

Tonka and Luke looked at each other, laughing. Even the kid who couldn't speak English was offering words of encouragement. The Enders prepared for the kick-off but the ref had already blown his whistle. Luke's goal was the last kick of the first-half.

'Great half, lads,' Jerome said brightly.

Each Ender refused a swig from the water bottle. Jerome watched quietly as they reached into his kit bag and produced bottles of Lucozade Sport and a bunch of bananas. Everyone was drinking and munching.

Jerome dug his hands into his tracksuit pockets. He decided to stand back and enjoy the glow of leading in a football match for the first time in five months.

'What's with the Lucozade?' he said.

'Isotonic. Keeps sugar level high,' Edgar replied, in between gulps of Lucozade Sport.

Jerome nodded his head, impressed by such a scientific answer. The boys seemed quite content to sit, eat and drink without interruption. But Jerome, spurred on by Luke's goal, was a hive of energy. He felt he should be doing something. Then it hit him, tactics for the second-half. This was a chance to sow up the game. It hit him like a megaton bomb.

'Right, we're changing to the hammerhead,' he said confidently.

'No,' the Enders, even Daniel, replied like a Broadway chorus line.

Jerome was about to question this organised insurrection from his players. But Luke was already on his feet, preparing to smooth things over with his blossoming man-management skills. Although in this case, it was more a question of manager-management.

'Boss. We wouldn't be winning now if you hadn't come up with this formation. It's brilliant.'

Luke glanced at his team-mates, urging them to offer vocal support to this statement. Jerome smiled as the chorus of 'yeah, boss,' and 'brilliant formation, boss,' rang out across the touchline. A sustained two minutes of praise was enough to stave off the dreaded hammerhead.

'Right. We stay the same, keep it tight,' Jerome said.

The Enders trotted out for the second-half, each one breathing a huge sigh of relief. Luke jogged across to David's side.

'Try and get the ball out wide,' he said.

David nodded his head. Luke walked forward to the centre-circle to kick-off with Ille. Valley Rangers came at the Stretford Enders like a team possessed in the second-half. They fought like tigers in midfield for possession and eventually got on top. Tonka was still untouchable, but he couldn't tackle four players on his own. An equaliser started to look inevitable.

Jerome stood on the touchline, nervously chewing his growing ball of gum as yet another corner was conceded. David Swayne was having an outstanding match, organising his back four, clearing his lines, one last-ditch tackle after another. But the whole defence was sticking to its task bravely.

Copper, Edgar, Alan and the Burke brothers were keeping Valley Rangers out. Every corner that came into the penalty area was headed clear, every shot a striker fired in was blocked.

The Enders had only been out of their half of the field on three occasions, but they were holding firm. As another timely David Swayne intervention prevented a certain goal, Luke could sense the heads drop on the Valley Rangers players. This was their chance to tie the game up.

'Lofty, look alive,' he said, without looking Lofty's way.

Alan Giles stood on the penalty spot. He bounced the ball off the ground three times before launching it into the air. He got good height and distance and Tonka won the header in the centre-circle, flicking it on towards Luke, ten yards inside the Rangers half.

As the ball came towards him, Luke didn't even stop to look before hammering it on the volley out wide left. The Rangers defence turned. It was a straight race for possession between Lofty and the No.2. Luke and Ille charged forward in support. They watched with baited breath as Lofty prepared to take his first touch.

He beat the No.2 to the ball and managed to flick it ahead of himself.

'Go on,' Jerome said, screaming.

Lofty had a clear run on goal. He powered forward into the left side of the penalty area. Ille and Luke were steaming into the six-yard box, waiting for a cross. But the expression on Lofty's face suggested he was going to try something stupid. Luke groaned as Lofty swung his left boot at the ball. Everyone watched in amazement as the ball screamed into the top corner, swerving wildly past the Rangers goalkeeper, almost bursting the net.

Jerome was in a frenzied state of rapture. He threw his bobble hat on the ground, then stomped it into the mud. He picked Daniel Popsecu clean into the air and danced about the touchline making a sound you normally hear from a sealion or a walrus when it's feeding time at the zoo.

Lofty O'Keefe trotted back to the centre-circle, one hand held aloft in an Alan Shearer-style celebration. Tonka screamed encouragement to his troops.

'It's not over yet. Concentration,' he said.

Luke and Ille chased the ball as Rangers kicked-off. But the game was as good as over. The Stretford Enders played out the last eight minutes in style. Luke could have grabbed a third but for a fine finger-tip save by the goalkeeper.

When the final whistle blew, everyone celebrated as if they had just thrashed Juventus 5–1 to win the European Cup Final. It was funny, Luke had played with the most success-ful schoolboy team in north Dublin, winning week in, week out. But in all that time, he could hardly remember a better feeling.

'Luke,' Jerome said, smiling happily.

Valley Rangers and the referee made their way off the pitch into the dressing rooms. It had started to drizzle, but the last thing on the mind of the Stretford Enders was getting wet. Jerome and Luke stood in the centre-circle, performing a barn dance.

The other players gathered round Jerome and Luke to join in with the celebration. They formed two separate lines, one behind Luke and one behind Jerome, waiting their turn in the centre.

Ille took Luke's place, Tonka took Jerome's place, so on and so forth. This dance of victory went on for several minutes, those not dancing clapped their hands and sang 'Here We Go, Here We Go'. The Stretford Enders were in the draw for Round Two of the league cup.

Cup Run

Luke stood at the pedestrian crossing on Main Street, his finger frozen on the WAIT button, staring at the man in the Opel Cadet. There was no doubt about it, it was his father, Jay.

Ella, standing beside Luke, glanced at him curiously.

'Luke, the lights are green?' she said.

Ella looked at Luke, concern covered her face. He looked like he was going to faint and fall over.

Luke stared at his father Jay who was stopped at the red traffic light. He wore a cream woollen sweater. His head was shaven and his skin was a healthy shade of brown. Suddenly the traffic light turned to green and the car passed off into the distance.

'Are you OK?' Ella said.

Luke could hear her clearly, but his lips were frozen in a slight parting. Ella gripped Luke's arm to stop him from falling over. He looked dreadfully weak, pale and unbalanced.

'Let's get a can of Coke,' she said gently.

Ella didn't wait for a reply and gently tugged Luke along the narrow pavement of Main Street towards Dorothy's Newsagents.

Until that moment, Tuesday had been a marvellous day ending in a glorious Spring evening. Perfect football weather. At six o'clock the Stretford Enders had taken to the field in good heart for their second round match against Ashwood Rovers.

They had streamrolled their opponents into the ground. Tonka had been the main source of inspiration, smashing an outstanding hat-trick from midfield. Luke, Lofty, Ille and Copper had had clear-cut chances to add to the score, but 3–0 was more than enough to set Luke smiling.

An hour later Luke almost skipped along Harbour Road and into the Bloomfield shopping centre. It was on a tide of unbridled bliss that Luke made his way up the escalator to visit J B Shaw's Model Supply Shop that evening.

Ella needed three tubes of Loctite Superglue 3 for the Spitfire. Who should pay for supplies had become an awkward point of contention between them. But Luke was in such a happy frame of mind after the match he decided to buy the glue and present it to Ella before registration on Wednesday morning.

Luke walked into J B Shaw's. Ella was standing by the counter. He stood beside her for a moment before she noticed he was there. When she saw him her expression changed from mildly happy to surly and cold.

Luke smiled, he was about to make her day.

'Great minds think alike,' Luke said happily.

He lay a five-pound note on the counter. The shop assistant darted his thin blue eyes between Luke and Ella, searching for explanation or instruction. Although she made no physical or verbal signal to the assistant, Ella didn't stop him from snatching the five-pound note off the counter and packing the tubes of glue into a small brown paper bag.

'We won tonight,' Luke said to Ella as they walked from J B Shaw's.

Ella gave Luke a fleeting glance but was obviously in no mood for idle chit-chat. Luke's shoulder slumped slightly.

They both stepped onto the escalator and stood in bleak silence as it slowly transported them to the ground floor. Ella's cool expression and unmannerly silence would normally have infuriated Luke. But not tonight. The high of the Stretford Enders' emphatic victory would keep him smiling for days. Still. He wished they wouldn't be parting on the other side of Main Street. Sadly, he pressed the button for the little green man.

'See you tomorrow,' Luke said.

And it was then it happened. Just as the little green man flickered on, and Ella was ready to move, the Opel Cadet slid to a halt at the red light with Luke's father in the front seat.

Now Luke stood there, looking like a little lost boy.

'Luke, the light's green,' Ella said.

She glanced at him impatiently as the green man shone and the other pedestrians crossed. Luke resembled a stone statue. Ella looked concerned. She followed Luke's glance to the man in the Opel Cadet. The resemblance was obvious. The eyes, the lips, the nose, even the dimples on his cheeks. Luke was staring at his father. Ella thought back to Luke's bedroom the day she collected the parts list for the Spitfire. Mugs of tea, the trip to Iceland, Jay's record collection. Luke had frozen to the spot that day at the mere mention of his father. Although she was still mad at him, now wasn't the time to hold a grudge. Ella gently grabbed hold of Luke's arm. What was needed was a can of Coke and a heart to heart.

It wasn't the same Luke Farrell sitting beside Ella on Dun Laoghaire harbour, sipping from a can of Coke. The intake of sugar steadied his nerves, but he was still to utter a word. Ella set her unopened can of Diet Coke on the harbour wall.

'That was your father?' she said softly.

Luke trained his eyes on the ground. For a moment he felt like talking, but every time he opened his mouth to speak, his brain went blank. Luke stared at Ella. For the first time since they'd known one another, Ella wore a sympathetic smile.

'You can talk to me,' she said supportively.

Although he couldn't say it, Luke appreciated her being there. But he couldn't go through with it. He slugged the drains of his can and flung it into a nearby litter bin.

'Thanks for the can,' Luke said as he walked off.

Ella watched him go. She knew better than most people when someone wanted to be left alone. Luke stumbled across the harbour bridge and onto Montague Avenue.

For the first time, Ella could see behind the macho lad who single-handedly tackled Swayne and Casey on her behalf. Behind the fearless football hero was a vulnerable and confused little boy.

Mrs Hendy poured two steaming cups of tea. She pushed a jam doughnut firmly towards Luke.

'Sugar's good for the shock,' she said with the bright, brisk voice of the nurse she had been.

Mrs Hendy sat down in her armchair. She studied Luke carefully. Ten minutes ago he had tapped at the sitting-room door. He hadn't seemed sure of what he wanted. She wasn't one to pry, so she had sat him down, filled him with tea and cake and waited for him to tell her what was on his mind. On the second doughnut it had all spilled out, how his father left when he was seven, how Martina never spoke about him, and how he had just seen him at the traffic lights in Dun Laoghaire.

Now he sat on the sofa curled up like a frightened hedgehog coming out of a coma, covered in crumbs. But Mrs

Hendy noticed he was cheering up. 'Thank God for jam doughnuts,' she thought.

'Luke, you must tell your mother as soon as she arrives home,' Mrs Hendy said firmly.

Luke chewed earnestly. Suddenly he felt a bit of a fool. Two women, Ella and Mrs Hendy, had seen him wandering about like an aimless zombie. But he hadn't been able to help himself. The sight of Jay had hit him like a round from a shotgun, straight through the stomach, knocking him clean off his feet. Some of his stomach was still missing. Still, there was room for another jam doughnut. He stuffed it in his mouth and got to his feet.

'Fanks Misses Endy,' Luke said, his mouth clogged with sticky, doughy pieces.

Mrs Hendy followed Luke out the back parlour door.

'Are you sure you'll be all right on your own?' she said.

He nodded his head gently and walked from the back parlour. Mrs Hendy stood in the hallway and watched Luke slowly climb the staircase.

Martina arrived home from college at quarter past eleven. Luke was sitting at the Packard Bell PC, pretending to care about the fortunes of Celtic in Championship Manager 2.

'Hi,' Martina said.

Luke didn't reply. He watched in silence as Martina went about the living room, depositing her books and folders on the couch and her bag on the table.

'Did you win tonight?' Martina said as she passed into the kitchen.

Luke didn't reply.

'Luke?' Martina said from the kitchen. Luke turned to face his mother as she wandered in from the kitchen, clutching a carton of orange juice.

'Use a glass,' Luke said quietly.

Martina sighed in her exaggerated way.

'Excuse me.'

She went back into the kitchen, poured a glass of orange juice, returned the carton to the fridge and walked back into the living room. Luke studied her carefully as she gulped down half the glass.

'Well?' Martina said, having finished drinking.

Luke's expression was eerily calm. Martina realised something was wrong.

'What's the matter?' she said.

Luke looked at the PC monitor and casually clicked the mouse as he explained.

'I saw me da tonight.'

A deathly silence ensued. Martina slumped onto the arm of the couch. Out of the corner of his eye, Luke noticed her holding her stare on him. She didn't look away in shame. He felt awkward and uneasy. Even saying the words 'me da' made him feel uncomfortable. Jay was his father, but he was no longer the head of the family or Martina's husband. The only connection Jay Farrell had with them now was his part in creating Luke. In every sense, he was nothing more than a stranger.

'I'm sorry, Luke,' Martina said quietly.

Luke was in the process of closing down Windows 95 on the PC. Martina sat still, waiting patiently for a reply. As he stood up from the table and clicked the ON-OFF switch, Luke stared at his mother with a dispassionate expression.

'Why are you sorry?' Luke said before heading into his bedroom.

He closed the door firmly and lay on his bed. Martina sat in the shady darkness, in two minds whether she should follow. A strong maternal instinct told her not to push him on this issue. And although it was painful to do so, Martina switched off the lights and went to bed.

Martina lay awake for hours. The crimson glow of the digits on her alarm clock documented the achingly slow passage of time. As the minutes crawled by, the temptation to check on Luke became unbearable. However, Martina knew deep down the next move lay with her son. All she could do was wait.

It was after three when Martina finally fell asleep, but it didn't last long. The orange street lamps still shone brightly along Montague Avenue when a crackling noise disturbed her brief slumber. Martina slowly climbed out of bed and plucked her white cotton bath robe from a brass hook on the back of her bedroom door.

'Luke,' she said quietly as she stepped into the living room.

The house was silent, apart from a muffled sound creeping out from behind Luke's door. It was the record player. Martina crept closer to the door and listened carefully.

'Everton, Everton, We all love . . . Everton. One for all . . . All for one.'

Martina took a moment to remember. When Luke was three, Jay had taught him the words to the Everton FA Cup Final song. It became his party-piece at family gatherings. For the first six months after Jay left them, Luke would play the record every day. Eventually it became every other day, every other week, and then once a year. This was his cry for help.

Martina opened the bedroom door and walked inside. Luke sat on his bed, knees tucked into his chest. He watched his mother carefully as she lowered the volume on the record player and sat down beside him.

There was no need for words. Luke started to sob, Martina held him in her arms. Fixing strands of his brown hair, rocking back and forth gently. She actually felt guilty; this was the first time she'd cradled her son in years. The distance puberty puts between a mother and son is extreme. Martina realised this could be the last time she nursed her little boy.

Dawn was breaking when Luke fell asleep. Martina gently moved his head back onto a pillow and covered him with the duvet. She stood at the door of his bedroom for ten minutes, just watching him sleep.

Four hours later, as Luke zoomed past Martina out the front door in a desperate scramble to be on time for school, he stopped on the concrete steps, turned and gave her a smile. As far as Luke was concerned, the matter was closed. Martina watched him sprint up Montague Avenue. She sighed sadly, watching her little boy leave her side.

Everyone was on time, the mini-bus didn't break down and Jerome remembered the way to Maywood Park sports ground. But as the Stretford Enders prepared to take the field on Thursday evening, nerves were getting the better of every-one.

Maywood Wanderers had a massive crowd along to watch the match. There must have been close to a hundred people standing around the pitch, not to mention kids on bikes, and countless groups of teenage girls sitting behind the goal wolf-whistling. It was an atmosphere to rival the San Siro or the Nou Camp, playing in front of 100,000 people.

'Listen up. Concentrate on your game, forget about every-thing else,' Jerome said.

Luke walked onto the pitch. He knew who would handle the pressure and who would bottle it. Tonka, David and Copper looked composed. The others looked terrified.

Maywood Wanderers, wearing red jerseys, white shorts

and black socks, kicked off and immediately applied pressure on the Enders goal. The cheers of encouragement from the spectators drove them forward and they forced an early corner.

'Keeper's ball,' Alan said.

This time his call was justified. He leaped into the air, clutching the ball off the head of the Wanderers No.9. It was just the kind of confident start the Enders needed to make. Alan held the ball tight to his chest, waiting for his back four to move up the field. Suddenly he spotted Muffin Burke in space on the right wing, he gave him a shout.

'Muffin,' Alan said.

He attempted to roll the ball out to Muffin's feet. Unfortunately, Muffin wasn't concentrating and the Wanderers No.9 slipped in ahead of him to intercept. The crowd cheered as he powered towards goal.

The Enders back four scrambled to recover. It was Edgar who jumped in with a last gasp sliding tackle just inside the penalty area. He did win the ball, but sent the No.9 crashing to the ground.

'Penalty,' the crowd screamed.

The ref waved away the No.9's protests. This caused uproar on the touchline. Jerome watched in despair as a rampant Wanderers, spurred on by the denial of a clear penalty, tore lumps out of the Enders. It was a miracle they weren't 5–0 up. But midway through the first-half the match was still scoreless.

A long clearance from David Swayne fell to Ille in the centre-circle. He laid the ball off to Tonka who prepared to knock a long ball over the top for Luke to chase. But before he could kick the ball, the Wanderers No.6's shoulder charged him to the floor.

'Referee,' Jerome said, shouting.

The ref waved play on. The Enders were in trouble. The Wanderers No.6 slid the ball out to the No.11 on the left wing. The No.11 then skinned Éclair Burke for pace. The crowd screamed as he swung a dangerous cross into the penalty area. David Swayne got his head to the ball, but his clearance landed right at the feet of the Wanderers No.10.

Copper Martin rushed out to charge down the shot but the No.10 managed to fire off a low drive which squeezed in between Alan Giles and his left-hand post. The crowd clapped and cheered as Alan picked the ball out of the net. Wanderers 1: Enders 0.

'Come on, lads,' Luke said, urging his team-mates onwards.

It was an empty gesture. Maywood Wanderers were like a steam-train rolling down a mountain. They ploughed forward at every opportunity and should have scored four more times before the half-time break.

'Concentration, lads. Keep it tight,' Jerome said.

He glanced at his watch, a minute into injury time. Luke and Tonka had dropped back into defence to help out their beleaguered team-mates. Ille was playing as a make-shift centre-forward, but he had hardly touched the ball.

Wanderers had yet another corner, their No.7 went across to take it. The ball came whizzing into the penalty area two feet off the ground. It was a badly taken corner, but in the panic Leslie Ward swung a boot at the ball, trying to clear his lines. It was a complete mis-hit, slicing past Alan Giles who was frozen to the spot. Wanderers 2: Enders 0.

The Enders trundled off the pitch at half-time with their heads bowed low. Jerome stood on the touchline, waiting for them impatiently. Everyone expected a scathing half-time talk from the manager, criticising their poor performance. But in contrast, Jerome talked in a soft and calm tone.

'Forget about it,' he said. 'It's gone now. We can't do anything about the first-half.'

Luke munched through his banana, listening to Jerome with the same focused attention the other players displayed.

'Two things. Pass it simple. Compete with them for every ball,' Jerome said.

He looked at his players, they all nodded their heads in agreement. Maywood Wanderers were lined out, waiting for Luke and Ille to walk into the centre-circle and kick off the second-half.

You could see it in the face of every Wanderer, as far as they were concerned, the match was over. They were home and dry. But Luke was starting to believe they could turn it round. Straight from the kick-off, the Enders knocked the ball about with purpose.

The crowd cheered and clapped every time a Wanderer got possession. But Tonka was winning it back straight away. It was an even contest, still 2–0 to the Wanderers, but a goal could change everything.

David Swayne broke down a Wanderers attack with a perfectly timed tackle on the edge of his own penalty area. He moved out of defence calmly, with the ball at his feet, before slipping a simple ten-yard pass towards Tonka. The Wanderers No.8 snapped at his heels. But Tonka held him off well before passing out to Ille on the left wing.

Ille hit a first-time ball to Luke, who was marked tightly by the Wanderers No.5. Leslie and Lofty were the only other Enders players in the Wanderers half. Luke had to hold the ball up for support to arrive. He shielded it away from the feet of the No.5, who eventually lost his patience and tackled him from behind.

The ref blew for a free-kick.

'Push up,' Jerome shouted, signalling his players forward with a frantic wave of his left arm.

Copper and Edgar moved onto the half-way line. David Swayne moved ahead of them to take the free-kick. This was a definite chance. David whacked the ball high into the penalty area. Tonka rose majestically above the Wanderers defence and headed it towards goal.

Luke had a split-second decision to make. The ball was still hanging in the air. If he threw his head at it he could knock it past the advancing goalie. But he could also get a fist in the face for his trouble. Luke went for it, throwing his head at the ball. He managed to knock it into the net but received a punch in the face and a kick to the ribs for his trouble. Wanderers 2: Enders 1.

Tonka went across to separate Luke from the crumpled pile of bodies which included the keeper and the Wanderers No.5.

'You OK?' he said.

Luke could see three different sets of Tonka in front of him but wasted no time in nodding his head. The crowd had fallen silent and the Enders were back in the game. By the time the Wanderers kicked off, Luke was starting to see one of everything again.

The match was there for the taking. The Wanderers became frustrated as David marshalled his defence tightly. Slowly the momentum swung back towards the Enders, but with three minutes left, they were still a goal down.

Leslie hassled the right back into a mistake outside his penalty area. His pressure paid off and the Enders won a corner. David came forward to swing it in. Luke knew this was their last chance to save the game.

Jerome stood on the touchline, biting what little was left

of his fingernails. David hit a poor corner to the near post, the No.5 heading it clear. The crowd roared as the Wanderers No.9 picked up the loose ball outside his own penalty area. He had a one-on-one with Edgar O'Lone, who stood between him and a clear run on goal.

At a time of great need, Edgar dived in with a brave block tackle to win the ball back. Copper Martin picked up the loose ball and chipped it back into the crowded penalty area. Luke was in the middle of a pack of players, with his back to goal. But somehow he got his head on the ball and flicked a looping header over the keeper's despairing dive. Wanderers 2: Enders 2.

'Yeeessssss,' Jerome said, screaming in delight.

The Enders piled on top of Luke in celebration. It was the last minute of normal time. The match was all but over, but they had saved it.

'Concentration, Enders, concentration,' Jerome said loudly as his players trotted back towards their own half.

The crowd were in complete silence as the Wanderers kicked-off. Tonka charged forward. He quickly robbed the ball from the No.7 in the centre-circle. Luke was exhausted, but he sensed a chance to win it.

'Tonka,' he said, screaming.

Tonka spotted Luke's run. He knocked the ball out onto the left wing, directly into Luke's path. He was forty yards from goal with four defenders in front of him, but Luke knew he could do it. He chipped the ball over the top, into the space behind the defenders. They turned and raced after it, but Luke had adrenaline on his side.

The keeper hesitated on his line, hoping his defenders would see off the danger. But Luke's blistering pace carried him clear. He picked up the ball on the left wing, eighteen yards out, and cut straight in towards goal. The keeper knew it was up to him to narrow the angle, but he had left it too late.

Luke hit an inch-perfect curler to the far post, beating the keeper's outstretched fingertips by the width of a razor-blade. The ball nestled in the back of the net, leaving Luke to sprint back down the touchline and dive onto the ground in a Jurgen Klinsman style celebration. Wanderers 2: Enders 3.

'Yesssss, yeessss, yesssssssss!' Jerome said, falling to his knees.

The match wasn't over yet. But the last minute and a half of injury time meant nothing. Maywood Wanderers walked off the pitch after the final whistle in a daze. They were unable to fathom what had happened in the final three minutes of the game.

Jerome would have felt sorry for them. However, his team's victory was the sweetest moment in his football career.

As the Stretford Enders left Maywood Sports ground that evening, they left as a team. Luke had scored a hat-trick, but the team had won the game. The victory meant a quarter-final tie against Brownstone Celtic, at home. But even if they lost the next game 7–0, no one could ever erase the memory of Maywood Wanderers 2: Stretford Enders 3.

Friday passed off in a flash for Luke and his fellow Enders. A series of in-depth discussions raged throughout the day on a variety of topics. The majestic comeback against Maywood, the upcoming quarter-final against Brownstone Celtic, the growing possibility of an appearance in the South Dublin league cup final. Almost overnight a sense of optimism abounded in the heart of every Ender. An optimism instilled within the space of seven days and three hard-fought victories.

When the final class bell rang out at four o'clock that

afternoon, Luke walked from Woodlawn Comprehensive with six team-mates by his side. It wasn't until they reached the narrow laneway that linked Woodlawn estate to Woodlawn Park that Luke remembered forgetting.

'Ah nuts,' he said aloud.

Luke turned 180 degrees and jogged away in a swift motion. Tonka, Copper, Alan, Edgar and the Burke brothers stopped to watch him go. The mountainous midfielder asked the obvious question.

'What's wrong?'

Luke kept jogging across the park but twisted sideways to answer Tonka.

'I left me history notes behind. That project's due in on Monday. I'll see you in the morning.'

Luke straightened up and continued across Woodlawn Park. He felt a little insulted that no one volunteered to jog back to the school with him. Then again, the reluctance of any schoolkid in the world to make unnecessary trips to school was quite understandable.

A lull in oncoming traffic allowed Luke to zip straight across Woodlawn Drive and make his way down the driveway. He counted only two cars in the teachers' car park. A red Lada estate that resembled an unusual piece of Lego, which belonged to Mr O'Shea, and a silver Ford Capri, which belonged to Mr Ambrose.

Luke entered through the main entrance and proceeded round the main corridor to his locker outside science room one on the far side of the building. He fiddled with the lock for a while, entering two unsuccessful combinations before consulting his school journal for the correct sequence.

'Thirty-three, fifteen, sixty-one,' he mumbled quietly.

With the locker opened, Luke retrieved his history

notebook and tucked it and his school journal safely inside his bag. He replaced the lock and continued along the main corridor that formed a neat rectangle back at the main entrance to the school.

On his way to the junction that separated the science and metalwork corridors, Luke saw a room door swing open up ahead. Ella appeared from the room alone.

Luke stopped immediately and took cover behind a row of lockers. He watched her walk to the junction and turn left, heading towards the main entrance. Only now did he decide to follow.

He moved out from his cover position and prepared to squeeze out an effortless 'alright' as he turned the corner. But before he could speak, a strange sight compelled him to silence.

Ella was standing ten feet away, outside the door of drama room one. She was staring at a large notice-board alongside. There were a number of small, black and white A4 posters pinned around the perimeter of the board, but the poster Ella was staring at with a blatant expression of sorrow, dominated the landscape of the whole wall.

It was a blanket-sized glossy with the *Starsearch 2000* emblem blazing across the top. Ella didn't seem to be reading the details. Luke sensed that she knew each and every word off by heart. He stood at the corner of the junction and observed quietly for a further three minutes.

At this point, Ella adjusted the strap of her schoolbag and exhaled a silent sigh. She wandered off towards the main entrance.

Luke didn't follow. Somehow the barely audible sound of her sigh rendered him useless. He was unable to move, unable to speak. He didn't completely understand the sensation of sympathy and guilt that zoomed round his gut but he knew it had something to do with Ella staring up at the poster. That was significant. Luke decided to find out why.

He moved briskly from his covert position at the corner to the main entrance. He was prepared to lend the same kind of emotional support Ella provided for him on Tuesday evening. He wasn't sure how, but he was determined to try.

Unfortunately, by the time Luke reached the teachers' car park, Ella had already jumped into the passenger seat of Jerome's bottle-green Ford Probe. Luke stood there and watched the sleek sports car zoom out onto Woodlawn Drive. It flickered briefly behind the camouflage of green railings and broad, brown tree trunks that lined the perimeter of the grounds before disappearing from view completely.

Without a further moment's hesitation, Luke turned back to investigate. He made his way inside the empty school building, populated now by a group of cleaners and the sound of their vacuums. The key to the entire mystery hung on the notice-board outside drama room one.

Luke studied the details of the poster carefully. He had walked past it countless times on his way to class but never really paid much attention. On closer inspection, he realised the poster was announcing a set of open auditions to find contestants for the show from the South Dublin area. 'All Welcome' it said. The auditions were taking place in Woodlawn Comprehensive over the course of three consecutive Saturdays. The ninth, sixteenth and twenty-third of . . .

'January,' Luke said aloud in surprise.

Maths had never been his strongest subject. But even he could put two and two together to come up with four.

Jimmy Greaves once said, 'Football is a funny old game.' Luke was starting to see the truth in this saying. Seven days before, the Enders had played Valley Rangers in front of no man and no dog.

Now, as they prepared to line out against Brownstone Celtic, Woodlawn Comprehensive school grounds were heaving with people. Everyone's relatives saw fit to jump on the victorious bandwagon and lend their fair-weather support to the Stretford Enders.

'Come on, Luke,' Cecilia said.

Martina smiled at the sound of Cecilia's encouragement. She looked across at Luke standing in the centre-circle. 'Who's that?' she mimed. He chose to ignore his mother, despite the fact she had taken the morning off work to watch him play.

'Hey, Luke. Who's that tool with your ma?' Tonka said, laughing.

Luke couldn't bear to look across, just in case he caught sight of Ronald's bright yellow tweed trousers. He threw a middle digit to Tonka, who continued to make fun.

'Snappy dresser,' he said, fighting back the urge to giggle.

'Come on the Celtic,' Peter Swayne said, yelling loudly.

Luke and Tonka glanced over to the far-side of the pitch. Swayne and Co smirked back. They had come along to watch the match in an effort to knock the Enders off their game. Dalkey United had already won their quarter-final. If the Enders could beat Brownstone Celtic, there was a good chance they would meet in the semi-final.

'I want them in the semi,' Tonka said.

'Let's worry about the quarter first,' Luke replied.

The ref blew his whistle and the match kicked off. Brownstone Celtic were a good side from Division C, but the Enders were on a roll. Swayne and Co's immature jibes acted as an incentive. They were quickly silenced as Tonka ran the show in midfield.

A sparkling Enders passing move from back to front, involving eight different players, left Luke in on goal. He smashed his shot into the top right-hand corner, but the keeper produced a phenomenal fingertip save to turn the ball over the crossbar.

The pattern of the first-half had been set. The Enders pressed forward, putting the Celtic defence under increasing pressure. Ille hit the post twice, while Luke made the keeper save on three separate occasions. As half-time arrived, Brownstone had yet to force a single corner.

'Well done, Luke,' Cecilia said as he trotted off the pitch.

Martina had seen enough. It was time to introduce herself to Cecilia. Luke was gulping down his Lucozade Sport when he noticed them deep in conversation. Martina waved to him, smiling happily.

'Is your leg all right?' a female voice said.

Luke turned round. A pretty woman in a white Adidas tracksuit with shoulder-length curly blonde hair smiled at him. She held a green first-aid box in her right hand.

'You got a knock on the thigh before half-time,' she said.

Luke recognised the woman from the photographs in Jerome's sitting room. It was Ella's mum.

'Mo, have a look at Alan's shoulder,' Jerome said.

Mo walked over to Alan Giles.

Luke recalled the story Ella had told him about how Jerome and Mo met in the casualty ward of Manchester General Hospital. He was in the reserves at Utd and she was studying to become a nurse. It was 10th March 1984, the same day Jerome damaged the cruciate ligaments in his left knee playing a reserve team fixture against Everton.

On the same day his football career ended, he fell in love. They were married four months later. Mo was now a matron in Temple Street children's hospital. Jerome had obviously borrowed her for the day as a makeshift physio.

Luke glanced about the crowd, looking for Ella. There was no sign of her.

As the Enders took to the pitch for the second-half, Martina and Cecilia were still buried deep in conversation. Ronald stood behind them. He looked like Lurch from *The Addams Family*. He noticed Luke staring over and raised his thumb in salute.

The second-half kicked off. The match quickly settled back into the pattern of the first-half. The Enders would attack, laying siege to the Celtic goal. Ille was on dazzling form, dancing around the defence time and time again. Tonka controlled the battle in midfield, while David kept the defence on their toes, ready for a Celtic counter-attack.

The match was heading for stalemate, and that meant extra-time. Of course, what the Enders had failed to consider was the possibility of a penalty shoot-out.

Luke realised it wasn't his day in front of goal as the match drifted into extra-time. He hit the woodwork on three more occasions. Tonka had a goal disallowed for handball and Leslie had a header cleared off the line.

Brownstone were playing for penalties, cheered on ably by Swayne and Co. As the heavens opened and the rain pelted down, Jerome and the Enders stood in the centre-circle, dishing out the penalty duties.

'OK. Who wants to take one?' the manager said.

All the hands went up in the air. Such confidence and bravery was a boost.

'OK. Luke, Tonka, Ille, Copper and David,' Jerome said.

It was a case of whoever held their nerve. The Brownstone Celtic players seemed quite relaxed about the shoot-out. They had played for it, defending bravely throughout the match. But if the Stretford Enders went out in such a cruel manner, they would only have themselves to blame.

Luke took the ball from the ref and strode forward to the penalty area under a hail of applause from the touchline.

'Come on, Luke,' Martina and Cecilia said in unison.

Luke didn't dare look across, but when he did, it wasn't at his mother. He noticed Mo massaging the stress from Jerome's shoulders. To his immediate left, Ella stood watching. Somehow, this sight made Luke feel confident.

He placed the ball on the penalty spot, walked back five yards and had a look. This was the time to pick a corner. Luke ran forward and smashed the ball low in the right-hand corner. The keeper dived the right way but was beaten by the pace of the shot. Enders 1: Celtic 0.

Celtic's No.9 smashed his penalty straight down the middle. Alan dived to his right. Enders 1: Celtic 1.

Tonka took the ball from the ref. He plonked it on the spot, walked back five yards, turned and hammered it into the top left-hand corner. The keeper stood still, looking at it. Enders 2: Celtic 1.

Celtic's No.11 looked cool, calm and collected. Alan Giles kept spitting on the palms of his gloves. He looked a bag of nerves. No.11 side-footed it high to the left. Alan dived to his right. Enders 2: Celtic 2.

Ille took the ball from the ref. He entertained the crowd with a series of flicks as he made his way to the penalty area. He placed the ball on the penalty spot, took six steps back, and ran. He hit the ball with the outside of his left boot, it swerved in off the left-hand upright. Jerome blew a sigh of relief as Ille jogged back to the centre-circle, hand in the air. Enders 3: Celtic 2.

Celtic's No.5 had been the lynch-pin of their defence. They wouldn't have reached a penalty shoot-out without him. He stepped forward calmly, placed the ball on the spot and blasted his shot low in the right-hand corner. Alan went to his left. Enders 3: Celtic 3.

Copper wasn't happy. He wanted to take a penalty, but he was nervous. He chewed on a fingernail as the ref handed him the ball. After placing the ball on the spot, he took an age before running up. When he did, he scuffed his shot low to the left. Swayne and Co cheered as it bobbled along the ground but somehow the Celtic keeper could only push the ball onto the post, it ricocheted into the net. The crowd groaned with relief. Copper smiled, wiping his forehead as he trotted back to the centre-circle. Enders 4: Celtic 3.

Celtic's No.3 took his time, trying to snatch a few extra inches by placing the ball on the forward edge of the penalty spot. He took a long run up and smacked it high to the right. Alan saw it all the way and dived into the air, clawing the ball round the post acrobatically with one hand. Enders 4: Celtic 3.

The crowd went wild, cheering and screaming in delight. Alan held his gloves high in celebration. Everyone was in rapture apart from David Swayne. Luke patted his left shoulder in support.

'Take your time,' he said quietly.

As David got to his feet and strolled forward, Peter Swayne and Co started a chorus of . . .

'Miss, miss, miss, miss.'

The ref walked across to Swayne and Co and told them in no uncertain terms where to go. Jerome couldn't help but comment.

'Leave him alone,' he said, roaring.

Brownstone Celtic's manager realised it was up to him to intervene. He walked over to Swayne and Co and with a quiet word sent them packing. It was top-notch sportsmanship, displaying the true nature of competition. Swayne and Co skulked off on their mountain bikes, leaving David to take the kick.

He stood face to face with the keeper. David made his choice. He would hit the ball low to the keeper's right. Halfway through his run up to the ball, he changed his mind. He side-footed the ball along the ground into the left-hand corner. The keeper dived to his right, but it seemed to take forever for the ball to bobble across the goal-line and hit the back of the net. Enders 5: Celtic 3.

It was all over. The pitch was invaded, the celebrations began.

'We did it, we did it,' Muffin said in disbelief.

He and his twin brother Éclair rolled about in the mud. Luke ran to David Swayne, rugby-tackling him to the ground from behind. Tonka, Ille, Lofty and Leslie, joined in and created a people mountain on the side of the pitch.

'See you in the semi-final,' Tonka said, shouting in delight.

Swayne and Co left the school grounds, muttering amongst themselves in disgust. It was a dark day for Dalkey United. The Stretford Enders had come a long way from the joke team everyone beat 5–0 and had a good laugh at. They were now serious contenders for the league cup.

Martina and Ronald ambushed Luke as soon as he appeared from the door of the dressing rooms.

'Congratulations,' Ronald said, offering Luke his hand.

He didn't want to shake it but Martina wouldn't let such rude behaviour go by without a severe punishment. Luke faked his most polite smile and shook Ronald's hand firmly.

Martina waited for the handshake to break before linking Luke's arm. She had that suggestive smile on her face. The smile that struck fear into his heart.

'I was talking with your little friend,' Martina said.

'What?' Luke replied fearfully.

Martina led Luke out into the open air. Cecilia stood on the nearby basketball court with her posse of friends in close attendance. It seemed like Martina was playing matchmaker. Ronald waited by her side like an obedient guide dog.

'Why don't you ask her out?' Martina said.

Luke summoned his most disapproving groan of embarrassment. He actually found himself looking at Ronald, as a fellow man, for some moral support. But Ronald was wearing an invisible collar and leash that led straight back to Martina's right hand.

'Take her to the cinema, my treat,' she said.

It was no longer a suggestion. Martina was now issuing orders at him. But Luke had just spent the happiest week of his life away from the hassle of female interference. Cecilia was beautiful, but was she worth it?

'Cecilia,' Martina said loudly.

This was a typical motherly trick. Fear of public humiliation trapped Luke in a corner like a rat. He had no option. He walked across to the basketball court. Cecilia smiled as he approached.

'Alright,' Luke said.

Cecilia waved over at Martina. Luke could feel an icy shudder running down his spine. Not only had he to contend with Martina, Ronald, Cecilia and her friends. Now his team-mates got in on the act, making kissy noises and the odd smart-arse comment as they passed by on their way out of the school grounds.

'I'm warning you, Farrell. Stay away from my sister,' Tonka said.

He held Alan Giles in front of him like a ventriloquist holds a dummy, framing him for the comment. The Enders broke up laughing, Luke responded with a lone mid-digit in their direction.

Cecilia seemed more than amused by the public attention their blossoming romance was drawing. After all, they were important people in Woodlawn Comprehensive. Why wouldn't the general public show an interest.

Cecilia turned back to Luke, who was desperate to get this over and done with.

'D'you wanna go the pictures?' he said wearily.

Cecilia made him wait ten long seconds before replying. 'OK.'

It took two short minutes to exchange details. In short, Luke agreed to call over to Cecilia's house on Elliot Road for seven o'clock that evening. Her father would drive them to the Stillorgan Cineplex where they would then decide on what movie to see.

Luke waved goodbye to Cecilia and her friends. He walked back over to Martina to report.

Over by the goalposts, Ella was helping Jerome and Mo take down the nets. Luke looked across at her. Immediately, she turned away from him. Jerome decided to crack a joke.

'Luke, in bed by eleven . . . alone.'

Mo slapped Jerome on the arm. He laughed it off and threw a roll of sellotape on top of her head like a plastic ring at a fairground.

Martina and Ronald made their way out of the school grounds, hand in hand. Luke trailed behind them in disgust. He wanted to stay behind and talk to Ella about the Spitfire. The last time they had spoken to one another was just after the game against St David's. But somehow he sensed she had no desire to start talking to him now.

*

Luke knew exactly what to expect. All the way from Woodlawn Drive to Bloomfield shopping centre, Martina talked endlessly about the big date. When she went back into work, Luke headed straight home, took a shower and got ready.

As expected, Martina arrived home early that evening to 'help' him get ready. Luke left the house at quarter to six, as soon as she arrived. He wasn't taking any chances. If he stayed there any longer she would be messing with his hair, suggesting he change clothes, spraying some of Ronald's dodgy Dutch aftershave on his neck.

Luke made his escape and wandered around the town centre for a half hour to kill time before catching the 46A.

Cecilia lived on Elliot Road, a cul-de-sac of four- and five-bedroomed houses that looked down onto the nearby Stillorgan dual carriageway. He reached her house for ten to seven. Thankfully the silver Mercedes was parked in the spacious front garden as a landmark.

Luke spun around, checking out the houses on Elliot Road. Semi-detached, double-glazed windows, huge front gardens, doors and porches, beautiful. But not just the houses. The pavements, the lawns, there wasn't one piece of litter in sight.

Luke pressed the doorbell and stood outside the porch. The front door opened. A short, slightly balding man with a well-maintained gut, wearing a light blue and yellow golf jumper above cream slacks and white sailing shoes, opened the front door. He stared at Luke for a while without saying a word.

'Cecilia,' the man said loudly.

It was Mr Giles, Cecilia's father. He looked at Luke with deeply suspicious eyes, as if he were trying to expose him as a liar or a thief.

'Come in,' Mr Giles said bluntly.

'Thanks,' Luke replied.

He took a tentative step inside the porch. That was far enough for Mr Giles, who maintained his position, blocking the doorway. He directed a focused stare at Luke, searching desperately for a sign of trouble.

Luke felt extremely uncomfortable and self-conscious, but he tried to smile it off. The sound of footsteps coming down the staircase was a huge relief.

'Alright,' Luke said.

Cecilia just smiled back. She looked great: white Adidas trainers, cream Levi combats, white belly-top. As Luke smiled, he realised Mr Giles was still staring at him with the intensity of a pneumatic drill.

Luke looked up, desperately wanting to fight back with a moody remark more becoming of a no-good northside ruffian. 'What's your problem?', 'Are you looking at something?'

'You ready?' Cecilia said.

Luke nodded his head. The porch door opened behind him.

'Alright, Luke,' Alan said.

It was a sight for sore eyes. Alan, David and Copper were standing outside. Three team-mates to fight his corner; surely this would tip the balance back in Luke's favour. However, his fellow Enders didn't waste much time in pleasantries. They had clubbed together to buy a two-litre bottle of Coke and two tubes of sour cream 'n' onion Pringles. They had also rented *Fifa 99* on the Playstation from Extra-vision.

'See you later,' Copper said.

He, Alan and David quickly moved inside from the cold, leaving Luke face to face with Mr Giles. It became very clear to him – all fathers hated to see their little girls growing up.

They directed most of this hatred back at the boys stupid enough to go on a date with their little girls.

As Cecilia took Luke by the hand and led him into the front garden, Mr Giles seemed to transmit a brainwave to him. 'I *will* kill you.'

The journey from Elliot Road to the Cineplex took five minutes by car. But it felt more like a transatlantic flight to New York for Luke. Once he was behind the steering wheel of the Mercedes, Mr Giles suddenly broke into life, bombarding Luke with question after question about his schoolwork, background, ambitions in life.

By the time they reached the Cineplex car park, Luke felt like confessing to whatever crime Mr Giles suspected him of committing. Mass murder, armed robbery, running an international drugs cartel.

'I'll be here for ten o'clock sharp,' Mr Giles said bluntly.

Cecilia kissed him on the cheek, then took Luke's right hand and led him inside the Cineplex.

'What's with all the questions?' Luke said.

'He was just trying to scare you,' Cecilia replied.

Although he let out a cool if somewhat arrogant, 'As if *he* could scare *me*,' Luke really felt like saying, 'It worked, OK? Tell him to stop.'

Cecilia led him inside the main doors of the Stillorgan Cineplex. Luke checked the back pocket of his Wrangler jeans to make sure he had the twenty-pound note Martina had given him after the match.

'Have you made up your mind?' he said.

They were standing in an ever-decreasing line of people steadily moving closer to the ticket box. Cecilia stared up at the information board displaying the movies on show in the Cineplex.

'I don't mind,' she said.

Luke nodded his head. He was completely unaware of how women delight in acting indecisive on a first date. As he scanned through the movies to find something where people got blown up, eaten, or blew other things up, Cecilia squeezed his hand gently.

'I'm glad you asked me out,' she said softly.

Luke smiled, he decided to be bold. He leant forward and kissed her on the lips.

'Me too,' he said.

Luke and Cecilia stood outside the main doors of the Stillorgan Cineplex. It was the fourth time that evening they'd enjoyed a long kissing session. Luke liked the kissing bit, it was the only way he could stop Cecilia from talking. All through the movie she went on and on. 'Who's he?' 'Is he that guy's brother?' 'Why are they in Miami?' The people sitting near them in screen three were groaning, shouting, 'Shut up,' and other less polite phrases.

Cecilia seemed completely unaware of the fact she was driving people insane. But the movie was paradise compared to the trip to McDonalds. *Star Search 2000* should have gone the whole hog and hired her as their chief P.R. officer. She never stopped talking about it.

Her plan for world domination included four consecutive Christmas No.1s (including duets with Ronan Keating and Madonna), Puff Daddy producing her second album, and a two-year stint as presenter of the MTV music awards. Luke stopped listening after that, all he could think about was Alan, Copper and David, eating Pringles, drinking Coke, playing *Fifa 99*. 'Lucky bas—' he thought to himself.

Three short angry beeps of the Mercedes car horn sounded more like a divine intervention. Luke broke off the kiss.

'Call me tomorrow,' Cecilia said.

Luke nodded his head, unable to answer with words. He watched Cecilia walk across the pavement to the passenger door of the silver Mercedes.

Mr Giles stared at him with a stronger, more intense hatred as Cecilia waved goodbye. Luke waited for the Mercedes to pull away from the kerb before walking down to the Stillorgan dual carriageway to wait for a 46A bus back to Dun Laoghaire. He wasn't sure if they were now boyfriend/girlfriend. But if Cecilia were to suddenly lose all interest in him, it wouldn't be the end of the world.

Luke sat alone on the bottom deck of the 46A. He looked out at the darkened mass of Sycamore Street passing by in a blur and he made a spontaneous decision. He jumped up and pressed the red button attached to the handrail to signal the bus driver to stop. He stepped off the 46A onto the saturated pavement outside Deegan's Volvo dealership.

Luke tucked his hands into the pockets of his black Adidas tracksuit top and jogged down the pavement.

'Luke,' Jerome said.

He opened the porch door and invited Luke inside. Jerome and Mo were in the living room, halfway through a late supper from Wong's Chinese takeaway. Jerome disappeared into the kitchen, leaving Luke and Mo alone.

'Are you hungry, Luke?' Mo said.

Luke was starving. He would usually bow his head and shyly mutter 'no' if offered food in someone else's house. But the sight and smell of prawn crackers and chicken balls was too good to resist. Jerome returned to the living room with a can of Coke.

'Get Luke a plate, Mo,' he said.

Mo stared up at her husband. Five seconds later Jerome decided to change his instruction.

'I mean, *I'll* get Luke a plate, Mo.'

Jerome smiled at his wife, desperate to avoid an argument about sexism and 'the taking me for granted speech' husbands feared so much. He walked back into the kitchen. Meanwhile Luke munched into a greasy chicken ball, dispensing with Martina's strict instructions on table manners in front of strangers.

Jerome came back into the living room seconds later with a plate and a fork. He shovelled some chicken chow mein onto the plate and sprinkled it with chips, curry sauce and a few prawn crackers.

'Thanks,' Luke said.

Jerome didn't bother to ask why he had called in to see them so late in the evening. He assumed it was to do with the semi-final draw.

Jerome turned down the sound on *Kenny Live* and propped his feet up on his foot stool.

'We got a tough one, Luke. Seaview Rovers, top of Division A,' he said.

Luke didn't seem that bothered. He was more interested in eating his food. Jerome grew impatient waiting for a reply.

'What do you think?' he said.

Luke looked up. He took a second to gulp down some curried chips before replying.

'We can beat them.'

Jerome smiled, delighted by Luke's confidence. Fear played no part in successful teams or players. Belief was everything in football; belief in your own ability. Luke continued with his meal, listening to Jerome relive a glorious reserve team game he played for Man Utd in 1982 when he marked Ian Rush out of the game.

'Of course, the scousers moaned that Rush wasn't fully fit. But he played against Benfica in the European Cup a week later,' Jerome said, smiling proudly before gulping down some Budweiser.

Mo was sitting behind him. She looked at Luke, mimed a yawn then made a motor-mouth signal with her hand.

'Oi,' Jerome said in protest, catching sight of Mo's hand signal.

Luke smiled. He had finished his food. Almost licking the flowers off the plate. It was getting late. Time to check up on the Spitfire.

'Is Ella about?' he said.

'She's out back, pottering away,' Mo replied proudly.

Luke got to his feet. Plate and fork in hand, he pointed towards the back garden.

'I need to find out what we got for English homework.'

Jerome was sipping from his bottle of Budweiser. He gestured him on with a wave of his hand. Luke took his fork, plate and empty can of Coke and headed into the kitchen.

'Thanks for the food, Mrs Barnes,' he said before passing through the partition doors.

'What you thanking her for? I paid for it,' Jerome replied.

Luke placed the fork and plate in the kitchen sink. He heard the sound of something soft, possibly a cushion, whacking against Jerome's head.

'You're welcome, love,' Mo said.

Luke closed the kitchen door behind him. The night air was freezing cold. He wasted no time and made a quick dash down the garden path to the rehearsal room. The Funky Starfish were nowhere to be seen. Luke assumed Saturday night was the night the Starfish set aside to party. He moved past a Marshall Amplifier and a Korg keyboard carefully, making sure not to knock anything over. He was about to knock on the door of Ella's repair room when he heard a sweet sound coming through the door.

It was his record, *Ella Fitzgerald Sings*. Luke stood back from the door and listened as the two Ella's performed a bewitching duet of 'Someone To Watch Over Me'. He took a seat on a Trace Elliot bass amplifier and listened without a care in the world. It was beautiful. It became difficult to separate the two voices, they blended into one like two flavours of melted ice-cream. Only a chance sighting at his watch forced Luke to move. It was twenty to eleven, Martina would be getting worried.

He snuck back across the rehearsal room, went out into the garden, waited for five seconds, then hammered loudly on the rehearsal room door. Twenty seconds later, Ella answered it.

'What?' she said angrily.

'I popped by to see the Spitfire,' Luke replied casually, strolling in without invitation.

The Spitfire sat on the repair table in all her glory. Completed, assembled and painted in her authentic RAF colours. Ella nudged Luke aside to resume work on the left wing.

'Is this it?' Luke said in amazement.

'No, this is one I made earlier,' Ella replied dryly.

'Can I bring her home?' he said in excitement.

'Not yet. I need to perform some tests with the engine,' Ella replied.

She looked up at Luke briefly, then returned to the job at hand.

'What are you doing out at this time?' she said.

'I had a date with Cecilia,' Luke replied casually.

There was a long period of silence. Ella ripped a white paper towel from a box of Kleenex on the table. She wiped her oily hands with the towel, scrunched it up, then stuffed it into Luke's chest.

'Throw that in the bin on your way out,' she said.

The towel had left a small smudgy oil stain on Luke's T-shirt.

'Wait a sec. When can I get the Spitfire?' he replied.

Ella turned her back on Luke, pouring all her attention into the wing. But he was staying put, waiting for a reply.

'Did you hear me?' he said firmly.

'Yes, I heard you,' said Ella. 'You'll get your stupid plane when I'm ready.'

Luke shook his head, tutted loudly and walked out of the repair room. It was a fact: women were a complete waste of time. In the past four weeks, the only time Luke felt stressed out was when he had to deal with women. It wasn't worth the hassle. He went back into the house, closed the kitchen door behind him, then looked out at the rehearsal room briefly.

'Moany cow,' he said quietly

Luke walked down the hallway towards the front door. He stopped outside the living room and swung the door open to say goodnight to Jerome.

'He's outside,' Mo said.

'Oh, OK. Thanks again for the food,' Luke replied.

Mo smiled. Luke closed the living room door and went outside.

Jerome was sitting in the driver's seat of his bottle-green Ford Probe, the engine was running. 'That's Entertainment' by The Jam blared out of the car stereo. Luke jumped into the passenger seat.

'I can get the bus,' he said.

Jerome didn't reply. He was too busy singing along with Paul Weller while reversing the Probe out onto Sycamore Street.

'I want to talk about set-pieces for next Saturday,' he said.

Luke would normally run a mile to avoid such a mundane conversation. But as Jerome spun out onto Sycamore Street, Luke was all ears. Football was better than girls any day of the week.

Luke wasn't sure how his team-mates felt. But all he could think about for the next seven days was the semi-final against Seaview Rovers. He had plenty of distractions throughout the week. Four separate hour-long phone conversations with Cecilia. Although the word 'conversation' was rather misleading. More like four hours of ear-ache.

If he heard one more thing about *Star Search 2000* he'd....argghhhh....#*%^$!!!

The dress rehearsal, the closing date for entries, the musical arrangement, Luke felt like he was presenting the show himself. Of course, the one thing Cecilia didn't tell him about *Star Search 2000*, was the most interesting fact.

Alan Giles set him straight on the gory details. It turned out the only reason Cecilia had passed the audition stage was down to their father, Dominic Giles. He was a senior editor in the RTE news department and a close personal friend of the executive producer of *Star Search 2000*. 'Did *you* think she was on the show because she was talented?' Alan said.

It seemed like the agony would go on and on forever. Every hour-long phone call from Cecilia was closely followed by a two-hour interrogation from Martina. 'What did she say?', 'Ahh', 'Then what did she say?', 'Ahh'. By Friday evening, Luke was starting to think Cecilia and Martina were impostors. Undercover government agents, hired by Seaview Rovers to brainwash him or drive him insane.

On top of all this, every time Luke approached Ella in school to ask about the Spitfire, she would either refuse to answer, or walk away. All these trials and tribulations would have caused Luke a searing headache, if it weren't for the semi-final.

THE STRETFORD ENDERS
VS
SEAVIEW ROVERS

Luke sat in the dressing room with his team-mates. No one said a word as they waited for Jerome to arrive. Luke glanced around the room. Even Ille and Daniel sat there silently. It seemed like nerves had crept in at the last minute.

'Sorry I'm late, lads,' Jerome said as he came through the door.

He slung the kit bag onto the treatment table in the centre of the dressing room. The boys waited for his nod of approval before digging their hands in for a jersey. Jerome folded his arms across his chest, then nodded his head to signal the go-ahead.

Éclair was the first player to dig into the kit bag.

'Sweet,' he said in delight.

Jerome had splashed out on a new kit for the semi-final. The faded Man Utd away kit was traded in for a royal blue Nike jersey, white Nike shorts and white Nike socks. Barnes' Sports Store was emblazoned across the front of the jersey in large white letters, but the cherry on top of the cake was the names and numbers on the backs.

Éclair took charge and dished out the jerseys. It was just the kind of pick-me-up the players needed. Man-management straight out of the Luke Farrell guidebook.

'Remember, lads. Forget who you're playing today. Concentrate on your own game,' Jerome said calmly.

Another managerial gem, perhaps he wasn't as inept as his hammerhead formation suggested.

As the Stretford Enders ran out onto the pitch, the large crowd gave a spirited cheer. Angela Burke had taken the day off work and closed down the flagship family bakery in Bloomfield shopping centre to come and see her slim-line sons take the field. Tonka's father turned off the grindstone for a couple of hours. Mr and Mrs Popsecu, Daniel and Ille's parents, stood on the touchline, clapping proudly.

'Come on, Luke,' Cecilia said.

She didn't bother bringing her usual army of followers to the semi-final. She had Martina to stand beside now. Ronald stood behind them like a bodyguard or a butler. Luke stood in the centre-circle. He shook hands with the Seaview captain and called heads. As the referee tossed the coin in the air, he looked about the touchline for a sign of Ella.

'Change round,' the ref said.

Luke snapped out of his self-induced daze and waved his hand, signalling for the Enders to swap ends. Seaview Rovers wore an all-white kit. They looked like strong, fit players and seeing as they led Division A, they would have to be skilful.

The match kicked off, Luke knocking the ball back to Tonka. Immediately, the Rovers captain, No.8, closed him down in a flash. Tonka tried to lay the ball off to Ille, but the No.8 intercepted the pass. From that moment onwards Seaview Rovers took the game by the scruff of the neck.

The Enders midfield worked hard to win back possession, but Rovers passed it so precisely, it led to the odd late tackle. This meant conceding dangerous free-kicks outside the penalty area.

'Tonka, get stuck in,' Jerome said shouting.

Rovers were in control of the game. But the Enders back four, brilliantly drilled by sweeper David Swayne, held firm. The fitness and stamina gained from a solid month of five-mile runs was paying off.

Luke quickly noticed that Seaview Rovers lacked a vital player in their line-up, a playmaker in midfielder. They had no one with the ability to dribble round a defence or provide a cutting-edge through-ball. This could be the key to the Enders survival.

'Alan, stay on your line,' David said calmly.

The Rovers No.7 swung in their fourth corner in a row. David rose above everyone, even Tonka, and headed the ball clear to the right wing.

'Give him a run, Les,' Jerome said, shouting.

Leslie heard this instruction. He knocked the ball fifteen yards past the Rovers left-full, forcing him to turn and enter a race for the ball. Leslie zoomed past him with ease. He kept his head down and side-footed the ball ahead of himself, moving deep into the Rovers half of the field. Most of the Rovers players were struggling to get back from the corner. This was a great chance to counter-attack. Luke and Ille were in the centre, two on two with the Rovers No.4 and 5.

'Les,' Luke said.

Leslie saw Luke drop off his marker and run towards him. He knew better than to ignore this movement. He side-footed the ball neatly towards Luke. As the ball rolled to him, Luke could sense the No.4 coming out to tackle him. He dummied the ball through his legs and spun, wrong-footing the No.4 completely.

It was now two on one and Luke had a decision to make. He could shoot, but on his weaker left foot. Before he could decide, the Rovers No.5 made his mind up for him. He left Ille unmarked to come and tackle Luke. Fatal mistake.

Luke slipped the ball past the advancing No.5, leaving Ille one on one with the keeper. He dashed out in a flash and spread himself big. But Ille kept his composure and neatly chipped the ball over the keeper's outstretched right glove into the back of the net. Enders 1: Rovers 0.

Jerome didn't shout in celebration. He held it inside, knowing full well that this match was far from over. Luke spent the rest of the half in midfield, desperately trying to help out Tonka and Ille.

Rovers had stepped up another gear. This was a moment for the Enders defence to stand firm; they let no one down. Alan Giles produced five top-class saves. The Burke brothers kept tight to their men, while Edgar and Copper won everything that came near the penalty area.

Of course, the constant pressure meant the occasional slip-up. But David was on hand to clean up anything that crept by his back four. The half-time whistle was heaven sent. The Enders looked exhausted. Jerome threw each one a bottle of Lucozade Sport while Mo dished out the bananas.

'Look, keep going,' Jerome said, unable to elaborate.

There was nothing more to say. The rest of the game was a simple matter of surviving. It was up to Seaview Rovers to break them down.

'Tonka, drop deep, help out Copper and Edgar,' Luke said as they went back onto the pitch.

Tonka nodded his head. There was no need for words.

The second-half was an amazing football spectacle. Seaview Rovers threw everything at the Stretford Enders. Corner after corner, shot after shot, chance after chance went a-begging. With eight minutes of the second-half remaining, the Enders had yet to venture outside their own penalty area, let alone their own half. But they were hanging on. Ille, Leslie and Lofty all came back to help out the beleaguered back line.

'Come on,' David said, screaming.

He had stepped out of the shadows and produced an extraordinary display to lead the Enders to the brink of victory. The Rovers No.7 swung in yet another corner. Lofty got his head to it, knocking it out for a throw-in.

'How long, Mo?' Jerome said anxiously.

'Six minutes,' she replied.

Everyone on the touchline was affected by the tension. Even Cecilia and Martina had suspended their discussion about hair, make-up, shopping and clothes to watch and pray. The Rovers No.3 took the throw-in. He launched it long into the penalty area. Edgar went to head it clear, only to be nudged in the back by the Rovers No.9.

'Referee,' Jerome said, screaming for justice.

No whistle. The No.9 had the ball at his feet in the penalty area. Tonka blocked him from shooting at goal, but he couldn't tackle for fear of giving away a penalty.

The No.9 laid the ball back to the No.4 outside the penalty area. He clipped a cross to the back post. Muffin jumped with the No.10, but he couldn't prevent him from getting a header on target. It was bound for the top left-hand corner. Somehow, Alan got a mere fingertip to the ball. It was just enough to send it onto the crossbar, but as it rebounded, a desperate scramble ensued.

The Rovers No.8 collided with Copper as they challenged for the ball. As they fell to the ground, the ball hit off Copper's left knee and tumbled into the bottom left-hand corner of the goal. The Rovers players had their hands raised, ready to celebrate, when Ille swooped out of nowhere like Mighty Mouse. He stuck out a toe and somehow tipped the ball round the post for a corner.

Everyone crowded the referee. Rovers claimed the ball had crossed the line. The Enders argued Ille had got it clear. Things got heated, resulting in two yellow cards for protesting. It was all too much for the Rovers manager.

'Little Romanian bastard shouldn't be playing at all,' he said.

Jerome heard this outburst along with everyone else on the touchline. Daniel and Mo tried to hold him back but he was determined to walk across to the Rovers manager and offer an opinion to the contrary.

'Say one more word and you'll be leaving with your teeth in a bag,' Jerome replied.

The managers squared up to one another, violence about to ensue. The linesman intervened and the ref rushed across to sort it all out. The players watched this heated argument erupting on the touchline, trying to figure out what had gone on. The sight of the red card sending both managers from the field of play was baffling. But there were still four minutes left.

'Come on, lads, let's win this one for the boss,' Luke said.

It was a timely injection of energy into the weary limbs of each Ender. The Rovers No.11 swung in a corner, Tonka headed it clear. The Rovers No.8 picked up the ball outside the penalty area and crossed it back in, this time Copper booted it away to safety. It was at this point Luke knew they had the game won.

For the spectator, the five minutes of injury time must have been agony. Rovers went close on seven separate occasions. But out on the pitch, each and every Ender had a resolute belief they were in the league cup final. The ref blew the final whistle as Alan Giles whacked a goal kick towards the halfway line.

'We did it. We did it,' Tonka said in excitement.

He picked Luke up in an affectionate bear-hug. Seaview Rovers left the field of play without shaking hands. It was sad that victory came on such a sour note, but that's what happens to teams so accustomed to success when they finally face defeat. As Luke removed his jersey, Cecilia ran onto the pitch and hugged him.

'I'm so proud,' she said.

Luke smiled, but somehow doubted the sincerity in her statement. The Stretford Enders had reached the league cup final. Dalkey United had won the other semi-final and Swayne and Co would face their old club in the final.

Jerome came bursting out of the dressing room door to congratulate his players. He broke open a bottle of champagne that had been concealed in the kit bag. He allowed each player a generous swig. Luke gulped a mouthful down quickly, but he had no time to revel in the celebrations. Martina was laying on lunch for four.

Luke stared at Martina in disgust. He had warned her on ten separate occasions to avoid the topic of *Star Search 2000* like the plague. But oh no, after a box of Mr Kipling's apple pies and two pots of tea, Martina ignored Luke's advice completely and invited Cecilia to give them a sneak preview of her song.

'I made it through the wilderness . . . somehow I made it threu-uh-who.'

Cecilia 'just happened' to have her own backing tape in her bag and gladly performed 'Like a Virgin' for Luke, Martina and Ronald, with full dance routine, of course.

Luke and Ronald winced as Cecilia struggled to hit every

note in the song. There was no debating it, she just couldn't sing. She sounded like a strangled crow. It wasn't like she had a nice voice and maybe a small problem in reaching the high notes. Her voice sounded like someone shovelling gravel and sand into a cement mixer.

'Like a vir-gin, HEY!!! Touched for the very first time . . . Lika-vir-er-er-er-gin . . . Witcha heartbeat, next-to mine.'

Despite the torture of listening to Cecilia sing, Martina's little tea party had been a worthwhile experience for Luke. It allowed her and Ronald to witness first-hand, the talking phenomenon that was Cecilia Giles.

Even Martina struggled to get a word in edgeways. When Cecilia started to discuss her career, there was no pause to allow anyone to ask questions. It wasn't a conversation, it was an information announcement, a press release. Another person's input wasn't necessary.

'Good luck with the show,' Martina said.

Cecilia smiled sweetly.

'Thanks, but I don't need luck,' she replied arrogantly.

Luke gave Martina one of those 'I told you so' stares before closing the front door. He had to face another twenty-five minutes of Cecilia.

She insisted on Luke escorting her home. This meant a journey on the 46A up to the Stillorgan dual carriageway, then a walk to Elliot Road. It *was* a gentlemanly thing to do. But it was only four o'clock in the afternoon, surely she could survive the journey alone.

'Seaview Rovers were a good team,' Cecilia said as they waited at the bus stop on Montague Avenue.

'Yeah,' Luke replied blankly, his mind a million miles away.

'Scouts from the English teams are probably at their matches quite a lot.'

This was a sentence worthy of his attention. Luke looked at her, if only to make sure she had said those words. Cecilia smiled. She took hold of his right hand and ran the tip of her index fingernail across his palm.

'Maybe it's time you thought of your career,' she said softly.

Luke was stunned by her audacity. It seemed Cecilia's plans for world domination spread to him becoming a professional footballer. It had been his own dream since he could kick a football, but for pure and innocent reasons.

To score a hat-trick for Everton in an All-Merseyside FA Cup final. To play in the World Cup Finals for Ireland. Football was about fantasy. The Stretford Enders had gone from hopeless losers to league-cup finalists with a little hard work, luck and team spirit. But now Cecilia wanted him to abandon his friends and team-mates to further his, well, her dreams of stardom.

Luke didn't say another word to Cecilia. He sat beside her on the 46A and walked to Elliot Road in silence, nodding his head as she continued to chatter on.

'Call me tonight,' she said as she put her key in the front door.

'Yeah,' Luke replied quietly.

As he turned to leave the front garden, he heard a dull thud. Luke glanced up at Alan Giles, smiling and waving from the window above the porch. 'League cup final,' he seemed to mime. Luke smiled and waved goodbye. As he walked back to the 46A bus stop on the Stillorgan dual carriageway, he had a nasty taste in his mouth. A taste left by Cecilia.

Luke arrived back on Montague Avenue for five o'clock. It was one of those limbo days weather wise. The sky was broken into factions. Dark grey rainclouds and pockets of clear blue sky lining up side by side. At any moment it could lash rain or break out in glorious sunshine, all on the toss of a coin. Ella was waiting outside the front door of Mrs Hendy's house.

'Alright?' Luke said quietly.

'Congratulations,' Ella replied.

Luke nodded his head.

'Oh yeah. Thanks.'

They stood on the concrete steps, sharing an awkward moment of silence.

'Do you want to come in?' Luke said.

'No. I'm just dropping off,' Ella replied.

Luke followed her back down the concrete steps out onto the pavement of Montague Avenue. Mo Barnes sat behind the steering wheel of the canary yellow Nissan Micra. She got out of the car as Luke and Ella approached.

'Do you need a hand?' she said softly.

Ella shook her head to signal no. Mo opened the boot of the car. The Spitfire was sitting there, completed and ready to fly. Luke looked at Ella with a smile of gratitude. He was overcome with joy and didn't know what to say.

'Mum, hand me out that bag,' Ella said.

Mo reached into the back seat of the Micra and handed her a black record bag. She slung it over her left shoulder before taking hold of the right wing. Luke positioned his hands carefully beside the left wing and waited for an instruction from Ella.

'It's not heavy. But grip the wing gently,' she said.

Luke took a loose grip of the left wing and lifted the Spitfire into the air. Mo closed the boot and got back inside the car.

Luke and Ella walked sideways along the pavement,

carrying the Spitfire. When they reached the front door, they gently placed her on the ground. Luke opened the front door. They moved inside as quickly as possible, hoping to avoid bumping into Mrs Hendy and therefore spoiling the surprise.

'Thanks a lot,' Luke said.

They had placed the Spitfire on top of the chest of drawers in his bedroom. He was busy examining the majesty of the finished product while Ella removed the radio control handset, instruction manuals and parts list from her record bag.

'You need to ring this number,' she said.

Ella handed Luke a piece of paper.

'What is it?' he replied.

'An R/C enthusiasts' club in Dalkey. Don't fly the Spitfire until you get a lesson from an instructor.'

'How much will it cost?' Luke said.

'It's free,' Ella replied.

She pulled the *Ella Fitzgerald Sings* album out from the bag and handed it back to him. They stared at one another for a while before she quietly declared.

'We're even now.'

Ella put her hand on the doorknob.

'Is that it?' Luke said.

She looked back at him.

'What do you mean?'

Luke shrugged his shoulders.

'Can we be mates?' he said.

Ella said nothing. She left without saying another word.

'Ella.'

Luke chased after her, but Ella refused to stop and talk to him on the staircase. He had to move ahead of her and block her path through the front door before she would consider listening.

'Why are you doing this?' Luke said.

Ella looked at him, she went to say something but stopped halfway. They stood there in silence for a moment. It became clear she didn't want to talk. Luke stood back from the front door. Ella unbolted the lock, swung the door open and ran down the concrete steps. He left the door ajar, watching her jog down Montague Avenue and jump into the passenger seat of the Nissan Micra.

'You're letting all the heat out,' a voice said softly.

Luke looked behind him. Mrs Hendy stood there, smiling.

It had been a while since Luke and Mrs Hendy sat down in the back parlour for tea and cake. They had a lot of catching up to do. But the problem was, Luke didn't feel like talking. He sat there silently, scooping the cream out of his chocolate éclair with his baby finger.

'Is something wrong?' Mrs Hendy said.

Luke looked up at her. He shook his head.

'What is it?'

Mrs Hendy was the first person offering to listen to him in weeks. Luke decided to take advantage of such a rare opportunity.

'Ever since I joined the Enders, Ella doesn't want to know me,' he said.

Luke took a bite of his chocolate éclair as Mrs Hendy considered a word of advice.

'Are you sure it's the football team?' she said.

Luke stopped chewing, he swallowed. 'What do you mean?' he said.

'Maybe it's to do with something else,' Mrs Hendy replied. 'Or somebody else,' she added tellingly.

Luke locked eyes with the wise old woman. She was spelling it out for him plain and simple. It was obvious really, but Luke had never thought about it before. Ella had been avoiding him ever since Cecilia took an interest in the Stretford Enders. Everything made sense now. Ella insisting on completing the repairs alone. Ignoring him in school, refusing to attend the matches, it was all down to Cecilia.

Luke blew out a nervous sigh. He didn't know she felt that way.

'Mrs H, you're a genius,' he said.

He gulped down his tea, jumped up, kissed Mrs Hendy on the cheek and left the back parlour. It was time to make things right again. A brilliant plan had flashed into his head like a bolt of lightning. All he needed was a minidisc recorder, the Funky Starfish and an application form for *Star Search 2000*.

MAKING A DEMO

Luke wandered around the ground floor of Bloomfield shopping centre at ten past nine on Monday morning. He was growing increasingly paranoid about bumping into Martina. She worked in the office of Boots, nowhere near the shop-front. But knowing his luck, the day he skipped school would be the same day she decided on a stroll around the shopping centre.

Luke took the elevator to the first floor. He was on his way to Dixons Electrical Store.

'Hello,' Amanda said in surprise.

Luke smiled, winning her over with his cheeky boyish grin. Amanda was behind the counter of the sound recording section of Dixons. The shop was deserted, apart from two other members of staff. One of who was fixing a Duracell battery display while the other tuned all the TVs to Sky News.

'Can I ask a big favour?' Luke said.

'Anything for you, babe,' Amanda replied.

Luke took a deep breath. He was about to put that promise to the test.

It was five to one on Monday afternoon. Luke sat alone in metalwork room one while everyone else went off for lunch. Amanda had proven true to her word and allowed him to borrow a minidisc recorder from Dixons for twenty-four hours. He scribbled 'Ella 1' on the minidisc cassette label and slipped it into the recorder.

Ella was working beneath the bonnet of a lime green Golf GTI. Luke snuck into metalwork room two unnoticed and hid behind the teacher's desk. Carefully, he placed the microphone onto the desk and performed a test recording of 'Nothing Compares to You' by Sinead O'Connor, the song playing on the radio.

He fiddled with the volume control until he found a good level. Now it was time to wait. Luke had a plan, but it was all based on a long shot. A real million-to-one outsider. Twenty minutes of radio crackle, tools dropping on the ground, wrenches wrenching, drills drilling.

Luke yawned with boredom. This was a bad idea. His neck hurt, he had pins and needles in his hands and feet and his stomach was rumbling from hunger. Ella slid out from the Golf GTI, indicated by the sound of the trolley wheels scraping along the floor. Suddenly the radio went dead. Luke held his breath in quiet anticipation.

'Yes,' he said in an excited whisper.

'The Very Thought of You' by Ella Fitzgerald came out of the speakers. The two Ellas started their enchanting duet. Luke pressed record on the minidisc player and listened on the headphones. It was a wonderful sound. Ella could sing, *really* sing. Her voice had a smooth unruffled ease, in complete contrast to Cecilia's laboured squeals.

For the next twenty minutes, the two Ella's sang. 'Someone to Watch Over Me', 'Blue Skies', and 'Sunny Side of the Street'. The tape contained every song from the album Luke had allowed Ella to borrow. But then, something different came out of the speakers. The volume of the new song was low and Ella's voice became clear above the music.

'What is it?' Luke said to himself.

He had heard the song hundreds of times. Jay definitely had it in his record collection. But Luke just couldn't put his finger on it.

'Do I love you, my-o-my . . . River deep, mountain high, yeah, yeah, yeah.'

Luke smiled. 'River Deep, Mountain High' by Ike and Tina Turner.

'Perfect,' he said quietly.

Luke dropped into Dixons on Tuesday afternoon with the unharmed minidisc recorder and a daring kiss on the cheek for Amanda.

'Can't stop. In a hurry. Thanks,' he said.

He wasted no time on chit-chat and departed from Dixons with the haste of an escaping shoplifter. He had five days to make everything right.

In the six or seven hours Cecilia spent on the phone to Luke, she had made sure to tell him every minuscule detail to do with *Star Search 2000*. Most of the time, he hadn't bothered to listen. But the one important piece of information he'd stored in his brain was the closing date for entries. It was this Saturday at 2pm.

Luke spent forty minutes standing in the public phone box across the road from Ella's house on Sycamore Street. He killed the time reading *An Official History of Everton FC*. Every now and then he would look up to check the front garden of No.18. Finally he saw what he wanted.

Luke left the phone box and darted across the road, narrowly avoiding an onrushing 46A heading towards Harbour Road. His dangerous dash across Sycamore Street drew a furious beep of the bus horn. But he paid no attention and continued into the front garden.

'Are you a starfish?' he said.

Cedric, the pint-sized lead guitarist, turned round and looked at Luke.

'Why?' he replied.

Luke held a tape cassette in front of Cedric's face.

'I have a proposition.'

The Funky Starfish passed a curiously long cigarette between one another while Luke rewound the cassette on Isaac's Aiwa stereo. Cedric passed the cigarette to Isaac, who took a long hard drag and exhaled a plume of smoke before asking:

'What's all this about?'

Luke didn't reply. Instead, he pressed play on tape deck one and allowed the Starfish to hear for themselves. Ella's powerful rendition of 'River Deep, Mountain High' rang out across the rehearsal room. The Starfish were instantly impressed, even Isaac. Luke let the song come to an end before making his offer.

'I can get you on *Star Search 2000*,' he said.

This news inspired some excited facial expressions on the Starfish, but not everyone was bursting with enthusiasm.

'We don't do competitions,' Isaac replied arrogantly.

Luke was in no mood to deal with volatile artistic temperaments. He took the cassette out of the stereo and walked over to the Korg keyboard.

'What *do* you do?' Luke said.

Isaac got to his feet. He walked over to the Korg and unplugged the power socket before Luke could touch any of the keys.

'When we're ready to strike. We'll let the world know,' Isaac said.

Luke avoided eye contact with him. He looked instead

at Cedric and the others. They didn't seem to be in total agreement with their bass player. His plan to further the career of the Funky Starfish seemed vague. After all, they had been together for two and a half years but had yet to play a gig.

Isaac was determined to build their career through mystery, magic, legend and rumour. Entering talent competitions, making demo tapes, playing showcase gigs, this was the boring, conventional route to fame. The last thing The Funky Starfish could be called was boring.

However, Isaac's vision of the road to fame wasn't working so well in reality. The other Starfish had been meaning to say this to him for well over a year. But the fact he was a mate, a moody sod and he owned the rehearsal room and the P.A. system prevented them from voicing their concerns.

'So, what's your plan?' Luke said.

Before Isaac could reply, he interrupted.

' . . . Let me guess. "We don't need a plan".'

Isaac wasn't impressed. He had a good mind to throw Luke out onto the street. But Luke was leaving anyway. He opened the rehearsal room door, letting in a large chunk of daylight.

'By the way. The girl singing on the tape is your little sister,' Luke said.

He closed the rehearsal room door behind him and made his way out of 18 Sycamore Street. It was all part of the master plan. Luke was simply moving his man-management skills from football to music. As expected, Isaac came chasing after him.

'Wait a sec.'

Luke stopped as soon as he heard Isaac's desperate yell. He waited on the corner of Harbour Road, just after the roundabout. Isaac stood on the corner of Sycamore Street as a heavy line of traffic passed by. When the traffic cleared, he jogged across the road. He stared at Luke suspiciously before asking.

'What's the deal?'

Luke chewed his bottom lip a while. Cars continued to zoom past onto Harbour Road.

'Can you play "River Deep, Mountain High"?' he said.

Isaac nodded his head.

'Meet me outside Dixons. Tomorrow, 2pm.'

With that, Luke walked off down Harbour Road. Isaac stood still on the pavement, watching him disappear. It was ten seconds later before he thought of asking a question.

'Dixons? What for?' Isaac said.

Luke turned his head. He was smiling.

'2pm, don't be late.'

The Stretford Enders had a light training session in Woodlawn Park the night before the final. The match against Dalkey United was scheduled for Templelogue sports ground at 4pm. Jerome was refereeing a two touch five-a-side match. He banned any form of tackling, and the whole point of the exercise was keeping possession of the ball.

Luke played a neat one-two with Ille on the edge of the penalty area before slamming the ball past Alan in goal. As he went on a lap of honour, Luke spotted Isaac standing behind the left goalpost.

At the end of the training session. Luke walked up to Isaac, who had a blue sports bag over his shoulder.

'I taped Ella's vocal after the instrumental,' Isaac said.

He handed Luke a tape cassette marked *River Deep, Mountain High – The Funky Starfish*. Luke nodded his head, slipping the cassette into his tracksuit pocket.

'You didn't say anything to her?' he said.

Isaac shook his head. He handed Luke the blue sports

bag. Inside was a portable DAT machine and four microphones borrowed from Amanda (and Dixons) so the Starfish could record the track. He slung the sports bag over his shoulder.

'I'll give you a call,' Luke said.

Isaac nodded his head. He walked past him and headed across the pitch to Jerome in the centre-circle. Luke went over to the lads on the touchline. They were changing out of their boots and shorts to go home. He took the sports bag off his shoulder and handed it to Tonka.

'Give us a hand with that,' Luke said.

Tonka took a quick peak inside the bag. In the meantime, Jerome walked over to the lads with Isaac by his side.

'OK, lads. Bed by eleven, no drink, drugs or women,' he said.

'Luke's the one with all the groupies,' Copper replied.

The boys laid into Luke with a collection of jibes. Even Ille made the odd smart-arse comment, translated by Daniel for the other Enders to understand. The best remark came from Tonka, who had the sharpest sense of humour by far.

'Gilesy, your sister's swimming with a shark,' he said.

Alan looked at Luke with a peculiar smile. There was no doubt about it, he actually felt sorry for him. He knew *exactly* how annoying Cecilia could be.

Luke took all the jokes on the chin and soon enough he and Tonka were standing outside his front garden full of tombstones on Harbour Road.

Tonka handed Luke the blue sports bag.

'This is it. Time for Swayne to pay,' he said happily.

'Yeah,' Luke replied quietly.

Tonka could tell something was on his mind. But before he could ask, Luke said goodnight and headed down Harbour Road towards Montague Avenue. It would be a busy day tomorrow. Luke had a few things to deal with before he could think about the league cup final. First off, a trip to RTE studios in Donnybrook.

THE MORNING OF THE FINAL

All those hours of boredom on the phone with Cecilia were finally starting to pay off. Luke hopped on the 46A in Dun Laoghaire at half nine on Saturday morning. In his pocket was the tape showcasing the talents of Ella Barnes and the Funky Starfish. He wanted to get *Star Search 2000* out of the way early on in the day so he could concentrate on the match against Dalkey United.

Luke walked through the large RTE car park. He weaved his way through the cars, moving towards the main building which looked like a giant sugarcube covered in tinted windows. He stood in the lobby, looking for an information sign to do with *Star Search 2000* before asking at reception.

'Can I help you, son?' a voice said.

A grey-haired security guard stood beside Luke, hands behind his back.

'Emm. I'm looking for *Star Search 2000*,' he replied.

The security guard pointed to a long corridor on Luke's left that seemed to stretch on forever.

'Straight to the bottom. Turn left at the vending machine,' the guard said.

'Thanks,' Luke replied.

As he moved down the corridor the sound of telephones ringing, radios playing, and TVs blaring merged into one. Luke kept his eye on the vending machine. When the corridor came to an end, he turned left and noticed a large brown door straight ahead. A brass plaque bearing the name Starlight Productions hung over the door.

Luke walked up to the brown door. He stopped outside, wondering whether he should walk straight inside. A whole minute passed by with him standing still.

'Excuse me,' a voice said.

A tall blonde woman wearing a smart red business-suit walked past Luke and pushed the brown door open. She was carrying a video cassette and a black folder. Before it swung shut, he caught a glimpse of a small queue of people standing in front of a desk.

Luke took courage and walked inside. This was it, the set of *Star Search 2000*. He stood behind the tall blonde woman, last in a queue of four people. Two men were sitting behind the desk with clipboards and pens. While one would ask questions, the other seemed to be taking notes.

Luke was standing in the line for five minutes. The queue was now just the tall blonde woman and himself. Everything was going according to plan until he caught sight of a sign, perched on the desk.

NO UNSOLICITED TAPES.
ALL TAPES MUST BE
ACCOMPANINED
BY THE ARTISTS
OR THEIR MANAGEMENT.

The blonde woman was almost finished. Luke was next up.

'Next,' one of the men said.

Luke saw another woman come into the studio behind him. He took this opportunity to make his exit.

'Hey, kid,' the man said.

It was too late. Luke was already running back down the corridor.

Luke sat alone on the top deck of the 46A, trying to think of a plan B. The bus was caught in heavy traffic on the Stillorgan dual carriageway. It was twenty past eleven in the morning. He didn't have enough time to get Isaac and explain things. He needed someone to act as the manager of Ella and the Funky Starfish. Martina was in work, Mrs Hendy was too old, that left one other option.

Luke stood at the information desk in the lobby of Dun Laoghaire College. He pressed a black buzzer on the counter for service. A fat female receptionist with short blonde hair, who had been typing away at a computer keyboard furiously, glanced his way. She didn't look at all helpful.

'Excuse me. I need to speak with Ronald Van De Kieft,' he said.

The receptionist stopped typing, but she looked at Luke suspiciously.

'Who are you?' she said.

Luke sighed in frustration.

'I'm his girlfriend's son,' he replied.

The receptionist started typing again. She was doing this on purpose. Luke gently whacked his head on the wooden information counter, hoping somehow to draw a shred of sympathy.

'Please, just tell me,' he said, almost breaking into a sob.

'Room twelve,' the receptionist replied angrily.

Luke lifted his head and smiled at her.

'Nice one,' he said.

Dun Laoghaire College was one of the fastest growing third level schools in Ireland. Alongside its full-time degree courses, it ran the best adult education programme in the country. Ronald worked as a lecturer in Information Technology and Computer Programming. But his job also included maintenance of the computers.

Luke found Ronald alone in room twelve with his head in the belly of a Brother laser printer.

'Ronald,' he said firmly.

Luke's voice caught him off-guard and he proceeded to whack his head off the lid of the laser printer. Luke groaned in despair as Ronald rubbed the top of his skull. He was wearing blue tartan trousers, cream leather slip-on shoes, a Bugs Bunny silk shirt and a yellow-and-black polka-dot tie.

'Luke, what can I do for you?' he said, wearing his gormless but friendly smile.

Luke stared at Ronald with an optimistic grin. For once, his zany taste in clothing could prove an advantage.

Luke and Ronald walked down the long corridor towards the vending machine. Ronald held the demo tape in his right hand, trying to sort out the details in his head.

'OK. So the tape has an instrumental version, then a vocal version,' he said.

'Yeah,' Luke replied.

'Why?'

Luke stopped at the vending machine. He was starving hungry and went about buying a Yorkie bar.

'Erm . . . artistic differences,' he said.

Ronald nodded his head. He loosened the knot on his polka-dot tie a little and walked forward towards the brown door. Luke munched into his chocolate bar, hoping to calm his nerves with a sugar intake. Two other managers queued in front of them with tapes.

Luke glanced at his Casio watch: it was ten to two. They had made it just in time to beat the closing date for entries.

It was actually a minute past two o'clock when Ronald reached the front of the desk. The two men sitting behind it said nothing. They left it up to Ronald to start the introductions.

'Good afternoon, gentlemen. My name is Ronald Van De Kieft, agent to the stars.'

Ronald placed a laminated business card on the desk.

THE JUICY PIE STAR AGENCY

Mr Ronald Van De Kieft

AMSTERDAM'S No. 1 AGENT
FOR ACID JAZZ & R'N'B

The card was Ronald's idea. Before leaving Dun Laoghaire College he and Luke had sat down at a Dell PC and created a business card. It took twenty minutes to design and print the card on the Dell PC, and a further fifteen to laminate. But it made a positive impression on Gerald and Stephan, the two executive producers of *Star Search 2000*.

'OK, Mr Van De Kieft. What have you got for us?' Stephan said.

Ronald flipped the tape out of his shirt pocket with his right hand, trying to catch it stylishly with his left. Unfortunately, he fumbled the tape, leaving Gerald to stop it from falling on the floor. Luke cringed, but Gerald and Stephan were laughing.

'Keeping you on your toes, gentlemen,' Ronald said.

Thankfully, he managed to turn his blunder into a joke. Stephan popped the cassette into a tape deck on a portable stereo. He had a finger on the play button when Ronald leaned across and pressed pause.

'Before we start, gentlemen, I must explain something about Ella and The Funky Starfish.'

Gerald and Stephan placed their clipboards and pens on the table. They settled back in their chairs to listen with great interest. Ronald stood back from the desk, circled Luke like a preying shark and came back, leaning his hands on the edge of the desk.

'On stage, they are one. Off stage, not a civil word,' he said softly.

Stephan and Gerald looked at one another, then nodded their heads together, trying to hide their complete confusion. Stephan pressed play again. Ronald intervened with the pause button.

'The Starfish record alone. Ella records alone. On tape they are apart, on stage they are one.'

Ronald stood back from the desk. He nodded his head, giving Stephan the all-clear to press play. Luke and Ronald looked at one another as the instrumental version began. It was a 50-50 shot whether Stephan and Gerald bought such a wacky story. Either way, they were in with a shot. Now it was up to Ella and the Funky Starfish to impress.

Jerome stood outside the school gates. He kept moving his eyes from his watch, to the red Ford Transit mini-bus, to Woodlawn Drive. It was twenty past three. They couldn't wait any longer. He felt physically sick as he turned to the lads and broke the bad news.

'We'll have to go without him,' he said.

Jerome climbed into the driver's seat of the mini-bus and started the engine. The other Enders looked at one another in disbelief. They would have to play the league cup final with only ten players, minus their captain.

Meanwhile, Ronald was beeping his car horn like a madman. He was trying to get Luke back to Montague Avenue in time for the match. The problem being, they were stuck in a two-mile tailback on the Stillorgan dual carriageway.

'What time is kick-off?' Ronald said.

'Four,' Luke replied.

There was no way of sugar-coating the truth. It was already half three, it would take another twenty minutes to reach Montague Avenue to pick up his football kit. Another thirty to beat Saturday afternoon traffic across south Dublin to reach the Templelogue sports ground, and that was if everything went according to plan.

Luke held his hands over his nose and mouth like a fighter-pilot's oxygen mask. He was going to miss the league cup final. Ronald glanced across at him. He reached over his left hand and gently patted him on the right shoulder.

'I'm sorry, Luke,' Ronald said softly.

Luke glanced back at him. He didn't say anything in reply, but he nodded his head and broke into a slight smile. This was the first moment they'd shared when both would admit to being comfortable. There was no tension, just a sense of friendship.

Luke stared out the passenger window at the bank of cars and buses lined up beside them on the dual carriageway. It was just one of those things. Luke had to make a decision. Ella and The Funky Starfish or Jerome and The Stretford Enders. He had made his choice, now he had to live with it.

Ronald didn't abandon Luke in his hour of need. He drove him back to Montague Avenue, waited for him to collect his football gear and then raced across south Dublin in search of the Templelogue Sports Ground.

Luke had never been there before and naturally they got

lost along the way. It was well after five o'clock by the time they found the pitch.

Luke jumped out of the passenger door and ran across the grounds. When he saw the Stretford Enders, they weren't running about the pitch. They were sitting on the ground with faces as long as the River Nile. Jerome gave a tearful Ille a reassuring hug, while the captain of Dalkey United received the league cup trophy from the president of the South Dublin District League.

There was nothing to say. Luke faced his team-mates, and the hundred or so people who had turned up to support the Enders, in complete silence. Ella was standing beside Mo and Isaac. She shook her head in disgust. Jerome stepped forward, his right hand holding his chin in a quiet moment of thought.

'What happened?' he said softly.

'I'm sorry,' Luke replied.

Tonka got up off the ground. He threw an empty bottle of Lucozade Sport at Luke's feet as he passed by.

'Sorry isn't good enough,' he said.

Jerome agreed with his stand-in captain. Everyone did. Luke stood on the touchline while Ender after Ender walked past him. None of them uttering a single word, but each of them staring into his face with expressions of disappointment and disgust.

As the Enders departed the Templelogue Sports Ground, Luke caught a clear glimpse of the victorious Dalkey United team. Swayne and Co were celebrating their victory. Cecilia walked across to congratulate Swayne. It seemed like the wind of change blew for Cecilia depending on who was the winner and who was the loser.

Luke was the loser today. Swayne and Co were the winners.

'Hi,' Martina said.

She walked over to Luke and Ronald. She kissed Ronald on the lips, then turned her attention to her son.

'What happened?' she said.

Luke couldn't take his eyes off the glittering silver trophy, held aloft by Niall Casey.

'It's a long story,' he replied.

Martina wrapped her arms round Luke's shoulders and gave him a loving hug. It was a nice gesture, but it did nothing to remove the pain and sadness flooding the forward compartments of his heart.

'Come on. Let's go home,' Martina said.

As they headed back across the sports ground to Ronald's orange Citroën, a question popped inside Luke's head.

'What was the score?' he said.

'One nil,' Martina replied.

Luke was back to square one in Dun Laoghaire. He spent the next two weeks of school listening to Swayne and Co brag endlessly about their glorious triumph in the league cup final. Cecilia made her move from Luke to Swayne a permanent one, much to the delight of Mr Giles, who saw Peter as a far more worthy candidate for his daughter to be dating.

The Stretford Enders formed a pact of silence, excluding Luke from making any kind of apology. The season was over anyway, especially since Jerome withdrew the team from their remaining league programme.

Luke tried to tell the lads next season would be different. But the one question they needed answered was 'Why did you miss the final?' He had to keep the real reason a secret. This meant lying to his team-mates, or refusing to answer them. He had no choice but to choose the latter option.

Ella still had to sit beside Luke in class. But after a week spent trying to explain things to her before, during and after lessons, Mr Duffy suggested they swap seats. Luke was put next to Niall Casey. Normally Casey would've been as upset as Luke about this turn of events. But it gave him a wonderful chance to talk Luke through his spectacular winning goal in the league cup final.

Casey spent an entire Wednesday morning describing his winning goal over and over again. Luke tried to ignore him, but he was determined to rub it in. Swayne and Co cheered Casey on while Tonka, Alan and Copper shook their heads at Luke in disgust. Even as he left the main building on his way home for a quiet lunch, Casey couldn't let up.

'So I caught it on the half volley … Hey, Honchee, come back,' he said.

Swayne and Co fell about the bike-shed laughing as Luke headed along the driveway towards the school gates. After everything he'd been through in the last three months, for things to end like this was heartbreaking. He turned onto Woodlawn Drive, his eyes trained on the pavement in front of his feet.

'Luke,' a voice said.

He turned round. Ronald was standing on the other side of Woodlawn Drive, waiting for some heavy traffic to pass by before crossing. Luke made his way back to the school gates as Ronald jogged across the road in his brown leather sandals. He was wearing his brown khaki shorts and a lemon short-sleeve shirt.

'Shorts? Is it really that warm?' Luke said sarcastically.

Ronald had learned to ignore Luke's smart-arse comments about his taste in clothing. He held a brown envelope in his right hand.

'It came this morning,' Ronald said.

Luke took a moment before grasping the letter out of Ronald's hand. This was it, *Star Search 2000* had replied. In the next few seconds, things could get a whole lot worse, or slightly better. He ripped open the envelope and pulled out a white sheet of paper. It took ten seconds to sieve through the bullshit and find the news.

'We're in, we're in,' Luke said in excitement.

At last, a break in the rain clouds. He couldn't help himself. He gave Ronald a hug and they danced about the pavement screaming at the top of their lungs in celebration. The students of Woodlawn Comprehensive, not for the first time, found themselves staring at Luke Farrell in confusion. This time he didn't care. He answered their silent question.

'Yeah, we're dancing OK? Dancing,' Luke said, shouting with joy.

After the excitement died down, Luke said goodbye to Ronald and ran back into Woodlawn Comprehensive, clutching the letter for dear life. He headed straight for metalwork room two. When he arrived outside the door, he found it was locked. He went into metalwork room one, where Mr Ambrose was preparing to leave for lunch.

'Sir. Is Ella about?' Luke said.

Mr Ambrose walked across to the door, ushered him outside and locked the room.

'She went home for lunch today,' he said.

Luke didn't hang about. He sprinted off down the corridor, out of the main building and back out into the car park. It was a five-minute walk to the bottom of Sycamore Street, but Luke managed to get there in under two. Mainly because he was running like a prisoner breaking out of a maximum security prison.

He rang the doorbell. It was fifteen seconds (which felt like an eternity) before Mo answered the door.

'Is Ella there?' he said excitedly.

'Out back,' Mo replied.

Luke smiled as he came inside the porch. He held onto the letter like a winning lottery ticket and proclaimed to Mo, 'I'm gonna make everything better.'

Luke gave her no chance to ask questions. He was already running towards the kitchen door like a stampeding elephant. Ten seconds later, he stepped inside the rehearsal room. Suddenly it dawned on him. If he told Ella about *Star Search 2000*, she could quite easily tell him to get lost. He needed something better.

Luke stuffed the letter into his tracksuit pocket and cleared his throat. It was time to try a new approach.

'Ella,' he said.

The repair room door swung open.

'What do you want?' she replied quietly.

Luke couldn't think of words to explain everything. He wasn't good at spouting romantic stuff. It seemed a lot easier if he just kissed her.

Luke stepped closer to Ella. He stared into her eyes and then moved his head to the right. She was torn in two. Half of her wanted to pull her head back, shout, 'How dare you,' and 'Get Out,' then throw sharp objects at him. But the other half took control, closed her eyelids and pressed her lips against his.

As they kissed, Luke thought about his previous experience with Cecilia. When *they* kissed it was a way of shutting her up. But this kiss wasn't like that. He wanted to kiss Ella. But when it stopped, he wanted to talk to her about stuff. Football, music, the Spitfire. This kiss meant something. But it had to end.

Luke pulled away from her. Now was the time to explain the kiss with all that mushy romantic stuff.

'I don't like Cecilia,' he said shyly. 'I like you.'

Luke bowed his head as his cheeks reddened. Ella broke into a smile.

'Why did you go out with her?' she replied calmly.

Luke scratched the back of his head. It was a tricky question, and one that could land him in scalding hot water, depending on his answer. He didn't want to say she was beautiful. That was just asking for trouble. But suddenly it dawned on him, a plausible answer and an easy way out.

'I knew it would make Swayne jealous,' he said.

Ella walked forward, she took hold of his right hand. Luke lifted his gaze from the floor and suddenly they were staring into each other's eyes.

'Really?' she said.

He nodded his head. Ella smiled, now she looked at the floor.

'Why do you like me?' she said quietly.

Luke was starting to sweat. This was getting far too mushy for his liking.

'We talk about stuff. Footie, music, you know. I like talking to you,' he said.

Ella didn't look too pleased with his answer. It was the truth, but Luke quickly realised she wanted to hear that whole beautiful, sexy 'No, you're not fat' stuff.

'Anyway. You're much better looking than her,' he said.

That was more than enough for Ella. Luke smiled at her. She replied with another kiss.

Luke called into 18 Sycamore Street that Saturday afternoon to pick up Ella for their first official date. Jerome answered the front door. He didn't look at all happy.

'Alright, boss,' Luke said.

Jerome groaned like an angry polar bear but didn't reply.

He held the front door open, pointing his left arm towards the living room, inviting Luke inside. Jerome sat back down in his armchair and Luke took a seat on the couch. After two whole minutes the silence became unbearable. There was no sign of Mo or Ella, and no explanation of their absence to boot.

'Erm, I'm here to see Ella,' Luke said.

Jerome spun his attention away from the TV for a moment. It was an intense stare, something that would unnerve a cold-blooded CIA assassin, let alone a fourteen-year-old school-kid. He reached up to the mantle-piece and took something into his hand. He threw it across to Luke. It was a silver medal in a small cellophane bag. The inscription on the back read: *Runners-Up, S.D.L League Cup, U-14.*

'Thanks,' Luke said softly.

The living-room door swung open. Luke glanced up. Isaac was standing before him. 'Ready?' he mimed to Luke.

Luke held his left thumb up.

'Let's go, Pop,' Isaac said.

Jerome switched off the TV, laying the remote control to rest on the floor beside his armchair. He stretched out his massive arms and yawned like a sleepy grizzly bear. Slowly he got to his feet to follow Isaac into the hallway. Before he disappeared, he gave Luke a stern wag of his right index finger.

'If you mess her about,' he said.

'I won't,' Luke replied quickly.

They shared a momentary stare. Two weeks ago, Jerome would've been over the moon at the thought of Luke dating his daughter. He certainly wouldn't have felt the need to give him a stern word of warning. But his unexplained absence for the league cup final had affected Jerome deeply, he still couldn't bring himself to forgive and forget. Not without some kind of explanation.

'I'm throwing an end of season party for the lads tonight,' Jerome said.

He dug his right hand into the pocket of his tracksuit bottoms and handed Luke two tickets. He left the living room, closing the door after him.

Luke smiled as he looked at the tickets. The first was courtesy of Barnes' Sports Store. Free entry, free Quasar and free Bowling at the Stillorgan Bowl that evening. But before that, a mysterious sponsor of the league cup had sent the Stretford Enders tickets to watch a recording of *Star Search 2000*, as a reward for reaching the final.

'I'll be there,' Luke said quietly.

'Where are we going?' Ella said for the fourteenth time.

'It's a surprise,' Luke replied.

They were sitting together on the back seat of the bottom deck of the 46A heading towards Donnybrook. Ella had abandoned her dungarees, duffel coat and Doc Martins for a completely new look. Matching sky blue fleece jumper and mini-skirt, white Adidas canvas trainers. Luke looked at her and smiled. Mo had decided to treat Ella and brought her into the city centre on a shopping trip on Thursday afternoon.

No expense had been spared so Ella could splash out on a new outfit for her first real date with a boy. Luke had to comment on her new look. It wasn't part of any scheme, he just felt like saying it.

'You look lovely.'

He could feel his cheeks turn red. He gulped with embarrassment after making such a mushy compliment. But Ella smiled and gripped his right hand tightly. As the 46A zoomed along the dual carriageway towards Donnybrook bus depot, Luke noticed the towering broadcast tower and enormous satellite dish coming into view. He reached up to ring the red button.

'Why are we getting off here?' Ella said.

'It's a surprise,' Luke replied.

Ella wasn't smiling by the time they reached the brown door leading to the *Star Search 2000* studio. She stopped outside, folding her arms across her chest while Luke held the door open for her to walk through.

'Is this all a big joke?' she said angrily.

Before Luke could reply, Ella had stormed off towards the vending machine.

'Ella,' Luke said.

He chased after her and stopped her halfway down the corridor.

'Ha, ha. Very funny,' she said.

'What?' he replied.

'Pretend to like me. Then bring me out here to see that stupid bitch on her stupid talent show.'

'You've got it all wrong.'

Luke took Ella's hand. He looked into her eyes, gently removing her glasses from her face with his left hand.

'If you don't believe I like you, I can prove it. Just come into that studio for two minutes. I'll prove it to you,' he said.

Ella could still smell a rat. But she didn't want to believe Luke could be so cruel. He leaned across and kissed her. It didn't feel like a kiss put on for show. She closed her eyelids as he slipped her glasses back on. She took hold of his right hand and walked back towards the brown door.

As they entered the studio, technicians and cameramen were busy setting up lights and cameras. Luke brought Ella straight onto the set.

'Careful,' he said.

Ella had to watch her step as they crossed over a mountain of thick black and blue cables running along the floor. They made their way down a narrow corridor leading onto a stage. Ella got the shock of her life.

'Pop?' she said with quiet surprise.

Jerome stood staring at Luke and Ella in confusion. Isaac and the Funky Starfish were smiling.

Luke brought everyone together to explain.

'Surprise,' he said.

'What do you mean, "surprise"?' Jerome replied.

Luke pulled the letter from *Star Search 2000* out of his jacket pocket. He also had the cassette tape that got them past the audition. He handed the tape to Isaac, who popped it into his portable stereo.

'I sent a tape of Ella and the Funky Starfish,' Luke said. 'The closing date for entries was the same day as the cup final. I left plenty of time to get back for the match. But there was a bit of a snag. I needed someone to act as the band's agent. By the time I got back to Dun Laoghaire, then back to RTE, it was two o'clock. I had to make a choice. Ella or the cup final. I'm sorry.'

Jerome finished reading the letter. The Funky Starfish's instrumental version of 'River Deep, Mountain High' came to an end and Luke's bootleg recording of Ella from metal-work room two came on. He knew exactly what her reaction would be and jumped in ahead of her.

'Before you start cursing and throwing things. Let me say something,' he said. He held her right hand, smiled and looked her straight in the eyes. 'You can win. I believe in you.'

It took a while, but gradually Ella's frown melted away. Jerome stood beside Isaac, still confused by it all. He took hold of the portable stereo and placed his left ear next to a speaker. Isaac went across and tipped his little sister on the shoulder.

'We've forty minutes to dress rehearse,' he said.

Isaac handed Ella the lyrics on a song sheet. She smiled, then handed the sheet back to him. They walked onto the main stage together, joining the other members of the Funky Starfish to begin their dress rehearsal. Luke wore a smug grin of satisfaction. Jerome stood beside him, his left ear still trained on the stereo speaker.

'This is my Ella?' he said.

Star Search 2000, heat one, started recording at ten past six that evening. Luke sat beside Martina and Ronald in the first row of seats. Jerome, Mo and the Stretford Enders sat in the back row. It was time to mend that fence once and for all. Luke squeezed past Ronald, he walked up the steep flight of steps to have a word with his team-mates.

'What do you want?' Tonka said bluntly.

Luke looked at all the disillusioned faces.

'To say sorry,' he replied softly.

There was complete silence. Jerome had already explained Luke's absence for the league cup final to the lads. But missing the most important game in everyone's life to enter Ella and the Funky Starfish in *Star Search 2000* didn't explain why he should sacrifice his team-mates' chance of cup glory. It seemed like the wound would never heal.

'Sorry,' Luke said softly. He started to walk away.

'Luke,' Ille said.

Luke turned round. Ille smiled at him. He whispered something to Daniel.

'Thank you,' Daniel said.

Ille held his thumb aloft. Luke smiled at him before walking back down the steps. It started to seep into everyone else's mind. Tonka, Copper, Alan, Edgar, the Burke brothers, Leslie, Lofty and especially David Swayne. He may have lost them the cup final, but Luke Farrell had had a dramatic impact on everyone's life. Would the Stretford Enders even have a team, let alone a glorious cup run, without him?

'There's always next season,' Mo said to Jerome, gripping his hand tightly.

It brought home how petty they had become. Jerome looked at Mo, winked his left eye, kissed her on the forehead and got to his feet. He looked down at his players.

'Lads, follow me,' he said. 'Luke.'

Jerome shouted out loud, catching the attention of the entire studio audience, which included Swayne and Co. They were there to support Swayne's girlfriend who had been drawn in the same heat as Ella and the Funky Starfish. Luke stopped on the steps and waited for Jerome. The Stretford Enders followed on behind him.

'Pre-season training, fifth of July,' Jerome said, smiling.

He stuck out his right hand.

Luke smiled back at him. They shook hands. One by one the Enders came down to Luke, said thank you and shook his hand. The Burke brothers mentioned they had both reached their two stone target in weight loss. Edgar congratulated Luke on his visionary decision to play him as a centre-half. Leslie and Lofty were grateful for the chance to play at all.

Copper and Alan thanked Luke for saving the team. Ille and Daniel offered him a kiss on each cheek for his kindness and warmth. Tonka said nothing, instead choosing to give him a bear hug. David Swayne was last. He stuck out his right hand and smiled.

'Thanks for believing in me,' he said.

'Next season. League and cup double,' Luke replied.

The Enders were back in their seats just in time. The stage manager came out and gave audience members one last warning to take their seats. Luke sat in-between Ronald and Martina as the *Star Search 2000* theme tune came over the speakers. Paul Porter, the presenter of *Star Search 2000*, came running out on stage to present the show.

'Act three on tonight's show is an acid jazz band from Dun Laoghaire. Please put your hands together for . . . Ella and the Funky Starfish,' Paul Porter said.

The audience rose to their feet in appreciation, led by the enthusiastic cheers of the Stretford Enders and Luke. Martina clapped, but not with any great enthusiasm. Luke had noticed this attitude since the news of Cecilia's departure and Ella's arrival. He tipped Martina on the shoulder and whispered in her ear.

'I've made an effort. Will you do the same?'

Martina had no chance to reply verbally. Ella and the Funky Starfish were about to begin. She and Luke stared at one another, mother to son. A slight smile, a nod of her head and her right palm massaging his left hand seemed like a positive reply. Luke leaned forward and kissed her on the cheek.

Isaac nodded to the show's musical conductor. He and his orchestra were to accompany the Starfish. Luke caught Ella's eye and smiled.

The music started, a powerful orchestral arrangement backing up the Starfish. Ella came in after the musical intro, singing the way she could. Luke saw the reaction on Martina's face. Even if she had been lucky enough to escape the torture of Cecilia squealing 'Like A Virgin', she had to be impressed by Ella's powerful voice.

Jerome and Mo were on their feet. Dancing with pride and delight as their two children combined their talents and blew the audience away. Cecilia stood backstage watching. Her jaw dropped in disbelief at Ella's transformation.

'What's she doing here?' she said in disgust.

Mr Giles patted her shoulders supportively. 'Don't worry about her, sweetheart. You're twice as good,' he said.

It was a horrible sight. Ella and the Funky Starfish were bringing the house down. They would walk into the final with ease. Cecilia had the grave misfortune to follow on as the next act. All Mr Giles could think of was those old biblical movies starring Yul Brenner and Charlton Heston. It was like throwing a Christian into the coliseum with a pack of hungry lions.

The entire audience was on its feet now, apart from Swayne and Co. Ella had them in the palm of her hand. She was a great singer, and a natural performer. She walked across to Isaac as he played a short bass solo after the second chorus, running her fingers along his shoulders like a veteran cabaret singer.

'I love you baby, River Deep, Mountain High, yeah . . .'

Jerome and Mo started to laugh with joyous pride at Ella's confident swagger. As she tore into the last chorus, the grand finale, Ella locked eyes with Luke. For a moment, she was singing to him. No one else. It sent a sharp shiver of satisfaction down his spine.

Ella and the Funky Starfish brought their show-stopping performance to a dramatic conclusion leaving the audience to stand, cheer and wail in appreciation for two full minutes. Paul Porter placed his hands on Ella's shoulders after the applause died down to congratulate her and the Funky Starfish.

'Should we even bother going on?' he said to the audience.

It was impossible to hear Cecilia's wails of despair below the cries of 'No' from the studio audience. As the backing track to 'Like A Virgin' began, Jerome, Mo and Luke went backstage to congratulate Ella and the Funky Starfish. Ella headed straight for Luke with a hug, and Jerome and Mo had to satisfy themselves with Isaac.

'Quiet please. They're recording,' Mr Giles said bluntly.

Ella and Luke glanced up at a TV monitor as Cecilia went through her routine. It was scary how hard she was trying. The veins on her neck were popping out as she strained to sing in key. Her face was pale, drawn, but completely focused as she stared into camera one with the intensity of an axe-murdering psychopath. Unfortunately, this intense concentration led to a mishap on, or more precisely, off the stage.

'Aarrgh, my leg,' Cecilia said, crying.

Luke fought desperately hard to hold in the laughter as Mr Giles and Paul Porter ran to the side of the stage to help poor Cecilia off her arse. The crowd was stunned into silence and hushed whispers as she tried to stand up on her twisted ankle. She was determined to continue, but it was quite obvious she was in a lot of pain.

A hushed conference took place between the stage manager, Paul Porter and Mr Giles in front of the electronic scoreboard. It led to an announcement from Paul Porter, while Mr Giles carried a hysterical Cecilia from the stage kicking and screaming.

'Ladies and Gentlemen. Act four has been withdrawn.'

Luke and Ella stood watching as Mr Giles and Cecilia passed by them backstage.

'I thought she was doing really well,' Luke said.

It was the fifth of September, a Sunday. The sun was high in a clear blue afternoon sky. Luke and Mrs Hendy walked from the 33 bus stop down a rocky pathway leading to a spectacular view of Dublin Bay and the Irish Sea.

Luke picked up a smooth grey pebble from the ground and threw it out over the edge of the cliff. It plonked into the water.

'So, this is where your father would bring you?' Mrs Hendy said.

'Yeah,' Luke replied.

Mrs Hendy noticed a sound behind them. It was music, a song she knew from over fifty years back.

'Vera Lynn,' she said softly.

The sound drifted out over Howth Head into Dublin Bay. 'We'll Meet Again', one of the most famous songs from the 1940s and an anthem for the Allied army, navy and airforce in World War Two. The sound of Vera Lynn was drowned out with a peculiar buzzing noise. Suddenly, the Spitfire zoomed out over their heads, flying out over the cliff.

'Jimmy,' Mrs Hendy said quietly, a tear welling in her left eye.

'This is our tribute,' Luke said.

Mrs Hendy turned to him, tears streaming down her cheek. She touched his face gently with the wrinkled tips of her fingers.

'Thank you,' she said.

They sat down in the grass and watched as the Spitfire circled the cliff and flew out to sea. 'We'll Meet Again' had finished. There was a brief pause before 'The White Cliffs of Dover' started.

Luke glanced back up the hill. Ella waved her hand down at him briefly. She nudged the volume dial on her portable stereo up a notch and went back to the radio control, sending the Spitfire on a course straight into the sun.